Alyssa's
Desperate Plan

SARAH LAMB

Paperback ISBN: 978-1-960418-14-2
Large print ISBN: 978-1-960418-15-9

Contents

Dedication

For those who find life has thrown the unexpected at you, remember that there's something better ahead and you will find it.

Chapter 1

Deepwater, Missouri 1870s

"Yer too small on the top. I want a bigger woman."

Alyssa Moore felt her jaw drop. She blinked a few times trying to collect herself, then frowned. Had she misheard? Surely, she had.

She'd traveled for nearly a week to get to the town of Deepwater after accepting a match from the mail-order bride agency. They had a success rate of ninety-four percent, she'd been assured. A match and true love was promised to her just around the corner, with one Mr. Gerald Weatherbee.

Truthfully, she didn't care about the true love part, she just wanted security and stability. Which was apparently being yanked out from under her feet.

"What...did you say?" Alyssa's voice was hushed. She wasn't sure if she was shocked or angry or both.

"Yer..." the man waved his hands around, mimicking a crude shape of a woman's curves, "too small. I like my women big, like me."

"And what am I to do, then?" Alyssa asked. Humiliation burned through her. "We signed a contract."

"Ain't signed a marriage certificate," the man chuckled. "I'm within my right to reject you." He checked his pocketwatch and shook his head. "I've got another girl coming. Good luck." He snorted then. "You need it, as itty bitty as you are. Maybe you can find a husband who doesn't have good eyesight."

"Why, I never!" Alyssa gasped as the man hefted his bulk from the chair and left the room, a rather rank smell coming from him.

Perhaps she should be grateful. After all, marrying a pig farmer wasn't exactly what she wanted for herself, but choices were slim, the agency apologized. Had she not been so desperate, she'd have waited longer for someone better.

Now what was she to do? She wasn't married, had no money beyond a few dollars the agency had given her, and was stuck in this small town.

Alyssa closed her eyes for a moment, then opened them, straightened her shoulders, and snatched up her carpetbag. "I'll just contact the agency," she said, sounding more positive than she felt. "They'll set things right. Maybe this time, I'll find someone better. Who knows, this might turn out to be a fortunate situation."

The idea filled her with fortitude, and she strode out of the small shed that served as the stage station, and headed to the town beyond.

Then she stopped.

Who could help her get a message to the mail-order bride agency? How did they send letters in this town?

Biting her lip, she looked around. Thankfully, though the area was filled with tall pines and oaks, there was enough of a clearing where the town was so everything was out in the open. Deepwater wasn't large. She could likely find where to go.

Alyssa studied the area. Nearby appeared to be a café. A general store was close to it, as was a dressmaker and a shoemaker. There were other small buildings and she wasn't sure what they were, but they had signs out and large shop windows.

Taking a deep breath, Alyssa slowly walked down the street. She was so busy looking into each of the windows, hoping to spot a post office inside, she bumped into someone.

"Oh! I'm sorry," Alyssa said.

"Not a problem," a man replied.

He started to walk away when Alyssa called to him. "I need to send a letter. Do you know where I can do that?"

"Sure, we've got a post office," the man said, and pointed to a row of buildings.

Alyssa bit her lip. "I...I'm sorry. Which one?"

"The one with the blue door," the man said.

Nodding, Alyssa said, "Thank you," and continued. When she reached the building, there was a paper on the door. She squinted at it, then tried the handle. The door was locked. Frowning, she looked around.

"He'll be back soon, love," a woman called as she headed to the café. "Peter usually takes his lunch about now." She pointed to the sign. "He'll be back in about a half hour."

"Thank you," Alyssa said. She sighed in frustration. "Fine. I guess a half hour won't make much difference."

At the other end of the street, she could see a small patch of trees, and what appeared to be a stream. It looked like a nice place to rest. It was certainly better than hovering outside of the post office and drawing attention to herself. She was feeling self-conscious after being rejected.

As Alyssa walked toward the stream, in the distance she saw the man who'd just insulted her and put her into this unexpected position.

Anger bubbled up, fueling her steps with a speed she was surprised she could do in her long skirts. The stream drew closer in her anxiousness to hide, and she wondered if the water would be cool enough to calm her heated face, and clean enough to drink.

She was so focused on the water, Alyssa didn't notice anything else but the large, flat rock where she set her bag down. She knelt, leaning toward the water, and dipped her fingertips into the stream. It was just as she'd hoped. Cool and clear. It would likely taste that way too. She moved closer and was about to reach her cupped hands into the water when there was a shout, and she felt herself grabbed from behind.

Alyssa screamed, twisted away, and pitched forward. Just before she fell into the water, a pair of arms wrapped around her middle and pulled her back, dragging her onto the bank.

"Let me go!" she shrieked as she tried to regain her footing. "What are you doing?"

Alyssa struggled and then broke away as the arms loosened, and the bewildered expression of a man stared at her. He blinked and his mouth opened and closed, but nothing came out.

It was all too much. First, she'd been rejected. Now, some crazy man was trying to throw her into the stream! What was with this town? The sooner she got out of here the better. Alyssa's face grew hot with anger, and she crossed her arms over her chest. Her too small chest, evidently, and scowled.

"Well? I'm waiting for an answer," she snapped. "Why were you trying to push me into the stream? Is everyone in this town going to be horrible to me?"

Chapter 2

The woman in front of him looked furious, and Peter understood his mistake. He felt like a fool. How in the world had he let himself get so caught up in his imagination?

Peter shook his head and stammered, "I—I wasn't. I thought you—you were going to drown yourself."

"Drown myself? Why on earth would I do that?" the woman asked, tapping one of her small feet.

"I got carried away," he muttered, looking down at his shoes. "I was reading. And..." He backed away then, hoping that she wouldn't yell for help, thinking he was going to hurt her. "Sorry."

He turned to leave when the woman's hand shot out. She grabbed his arm and when he stopped and looked back at her, she froze. She had a look he'd seen before, when stumbling upon a startled animal in the woods. He opened his mouth to apologize again when she spoke first.

"I'm sorry," she said, her voice low. "It has been the worst of days, and I misunderstood your gesture. I'm Alyssa Moore."

"It's my fault completely," Peter said. He held out his hand. "Peter West. Postmaster."

"Postmaster?" Her face brightened. "Then you can help me."

"I'll gladly do whatever I can to make amends for what just happened," Peter said.

"I need someone to help me post an urgent letter," Miss Moore said. Then, she gave him a considering look. "But will you first tell me why you thought I was trying to drown myself?"

He shrugged, and felt his face grow warm. "I was reading," he stammered, and then pointed a short distance away to a book in the grass. "*Hamlet*. By Shakespeare?" At her head shake, he continued, "Well, I was at the part where Ophelia was distraught. She went into the water to kill herself. I suppose my imagination ran wild. I saw you kneel next to the water, and you were so fair, like she was, I didn't want you to…" he stopped. "I sound like a fool," he muttered, looking away.

"No, you don't," Miss Moore said. She gave him a small smile, and a warmth blossomed throughout him. "You sound very sweet. Polite. I appreciate that. I wasn't going to drown myself. I was just hot from being angry and thirsty. The stream seemed the perfect solution to both."

"The water is quite refreshing," Peter agreed. Then it was his turn to study her. "But why were you angry? You mentioned something about everyone in this town not being horrible. Has that really been the case for you?"

She nodded. "It has. Well," she paused, and shook her head. "Perhaps that's a slight exaggeration. Only one person has been. But that's why I need you to send the letter." She took a deep breath. "It's been a most upsetting day, and I'm concerned that I don't have the means to make it better."

"I will help however I can," Peter assured her. "I know a good number of people here who will also help."

"Maybe," she answered, looking doubtful.

There was a rustling in the brush and she tensed, looking that way. "Is there an animal hiding?" she whispered.

"Yes. In a manner of speaking," he answered, and let out a short whistle. His horse walked through the brush, looked at Peter lazily, and tore at the grass. Her dark coat shone in the sun, and Peter couldn't help but feel pride.

"Oh! He's beautiful! May I?" Miss Moore asked, moving toward the horse.

"Of course," Peter answered, pleased she liked her. "This is Velvet. She's mine."

"What a fine specimen," she cooed, reaching over to let the horse sniff her hand before she ran long fingers over the sleek neck. "She's stunning."

"Thank you," Peter answered. "Had her for a long time and keep her at the livery." He gestured back toward the town. "Shall we go? I'll open the post office and get your letter prepared."

"Yes, thank you," Miss Moore said. She went and picked up her carpetbag.

"I can—" he held out a hand, but she shook her head.

"No, thank you, I have it," she said. "Anyway, you have the horse."

They walked in silence. Peter hoped she didn't notice how slowly they were moving. When he went slower or when he rode, his limp didn't show. That's why he took Velvet as many places as he could if he had to go a distance. It kept his leg from aching and also masked his infirmary.

Though he was used to the stares some folk, especially the children, gave him, Miss Moore seemed to be new in town and he wanted to make a good impression on her for as long as she was here.

They soon reached the post office, and nearby the livery. "One moment," Peter said. "I just want to take Velvet to her stall. I'll be right back."

She nodded, and he felt her eyes on him as he walked the horse over, then returned. If she noticed his limp, she didn't say anything, and he felt his discomfort ease slightly when he unlocked the post office door.

Removing the sign he put up while he was at lunch, Peter made his way to the counter and stood behind it. "Now, you said a letter, correct?" he asked.

"Yes," she answered, then took a deep breath. "Or whatever other way would get a message to the Marston Mail-Order Bride Agency in Birchfield."

"Mail-order bride," he mumbled as he wrote down her words on an envelope. Then he looked up. "Would you like to do it?" he asked, offering her a sheet of paper and his pencil. "If it's something private, then I understand."

Miss Moore shook her head. "Would you?" she asked. She bit her lip, and he didn't miss her look of hesitation. "It is private," she said softly. "And terribly embarrassing. So, I would appreciate your confidence."

"Of course," Peter answered. He nodded, the pencil hovering over the paper. "I'm ready."

She took a deep breath, and Peter could see that Miss Moore was trying to gather her thoughts. Finally, she said, "Arrived at Deepwater and was rejected before marriage. Low on money, and not sure what to do. Contract was signed. Please advise."

Peter copied the words, swallowing hard. *Rejected? Her? Who would do such a thing! And why?* He wanted to ask the questions burning in him, but that wouldn't have been polite. There was a slight trembling of her lower lip, and her face was flushed red. So, he simply nodded, pushed the letter toward her and asked, "How's that?"

She simply nodded, not even looking down. "That'll be fine," she said softly. "Do you know of an inexpensive place I can stay until I wait for a reply?"

"We only have one place with rooms here," Peter said, as he put the letter into the envelope. "It's over at the café. Want me to walk you there?"

She hesitated, then looked out the window. "That building there, with the large glass window?" she asked.

"That's the one," he agreed.

"No, I can manage," she said.

Miss Moore took a deep breath and turned to leave. Then she turned back. "Can I ask you a question?" she asked.

"Of course," Peter said. His leg was starting to ache, and he slid his tall stool closer to sit.

"The girl who drowned. What did you say her name was?"

He was puzzled for a moment, then realized what she must have meant. His book. "Ophelia?" he asked.

"Yes. That's it. Why did she? What had happened? Was it an accident?" Her eyes were curious, and she waited almost anxiously to hear the answer.

"She was a noblewoman," he explained. "The man she loved, a prince, treated her cruelly. He said unkind things to her and even murdered her father. Eventually, she became mad. Couldn't handle the pain anymore. She was singing and picking flowers by the water, and just..." Peter finished with a shrug.

Miss Moore nodded, solemnly. "I see. I understand now. Thank you. I—I don't blame her then. To be used and treated cruelly is a terrible thing. Thank you, Postmaster West."

"P-Peter," he stammered. "Just Peter."

She smiled. "Then you must call me Alyssa." Her voice was soft as she spoke, and then she turned and left the post office.

Peter watched her depart, walking across the street to the café. With a sigh, he picked up her letter and moved to the mail sack. As he dropped it in, he wondered—who would reject a woman like her?

His imagination took wild again and he shuddered. She wouldn't think of drowning herself, would she? If she was upset? What if that mail-order agency didn't find her someone else? He was sure they would, and hoped it wouldn't be someone terrible. She deserved someone nice. Someone who would appreciate her.

A flurry of excitement filled him, and then an idea. He knew it was foolish. Ridiculous.

But what *would* happen if he just kept the letter for a few days? Got to know her more? Was there a chance she might stay? With...him?

Peter dug into the sack and pulled out her letter. He turned it over in his fingers and looked at it for a long moment. Mail came twice a week. If he missed tomorrow's mail, that wouldn't be so bad, would it? He tapped the letter in his palm as he looked at it.

Then he sighed deeply. Being dishonest wasn't who he was. She—just like everyone else—depended on him to see the letter delivered. That's just what he'd do, like it or not.

Reluctantly, Peter placed the letter in the mail sack. If they got to know each other, it would have to be by an honest way. Not him being deceptive.

Chapter 3

Feeling a little nervous, Alyssa pushed open the door to the café. A tiny bell chimed and a frizzy-haired woman popped out from around the corner. It was the same woman who had told her the post office was closed for lunch.

"Hello," she greeted warmly. "I'm Maggie. What can I do for you, hon?"

"I need a place to stay for a few days," Alyssa said. "There was a...mix up with the mail-order bride agency when I came to fulfill my side of the commitment. I'm waiting to hear back from them and figure out what I'm supposed to do."

"Of course," Maggie replied. "We've several nice rooms."

Alyssa flinched. "How nice? I apologize for being blunt, but I've very little money, and—"

"And that's not a problem at all," Maggie answered. "You'll find all my rooms are clean, you'll get your meals included, and it won't cost much." She walked over and squeezed Alyssa's arm. "Don't you worry. We'll discuss this upstairs, away from prying ears, eh?"

Alyssa looked around to see what prying ears might be nearby, but didn't see anyone else in the café. With a nod, she followed Maggie up the stairs.

"How about this one?" the woman asked.

Peering inside, Alyssa answered, "It's perfect! Thank you."

Soft green and blues filled the room. Alyssa let her fingers trail over a plush chair sitting next to a large window with lacy curtains. The bedspread, also blue and green, was a lovely rag quilt that spoke of a number of hours in its making. A small mirror hung over a washstand, and Alyssa sighed when she saw her weary face reflected in it. She looked just as exhausted as she felt.

What a day it had been. What would tomorrow be like? There was no time to ponder further. Maggie said, "Now that your bag is here, follow me downstairs. A strong cup of tea, a little cake, and that will set you to rights."

"That sounds good," Alyssa said appreciatively. She followed Maggie down the stairs, pausing only to close her bedroom door.

Downstairs, Alyssa sat at a small table near a window and let her gaze roam the small town. It was growing late in the afternoon. It was the time of year that shadows fell early. She wondered when the mail would come to take her letter to the mail-order bride agency. Would there be a reply soon? She hoped so.

Alyssa liked plans. She liked knowing what was going to happen and when. This suddenly unexpected and very unwelcome event had upset her.

"Here you are, dear," Maggie said, and slid a steaming cup to her. "Tomorrow, I'll have fresh apple cider too, if you like. It's quite popular around here."

"That sounds wonderful," Alyssa said. "Thank you." She took a sip and set her cup down, picking up the fork sitting next to a large slice of cake. Her mouth started to water.

Maggie sat across from her. "Tell me about yourself," she said. Then she frowned. "Hank, that's my husband, says I talk too much. That I'm nosy. But around here, though we are growing, all the news comes from travelers, and we are quite hungry for it. If I talk too much or ask too many questions, just tell me so."

"I've not much to tell," Alyssa said. "You know there was a mix up, and the man I was to wed, he, well..." Alyssa wanted to tell Maggie. There was something about her that put her at ease. In Maggie, she sensed she'd find both a sympathetic ear and a good friend, but her pride wouldn't let her. She instead offered a weak smile. "I wasn't what he expected, and by the looks of him, I'm quite glad.

However, that does put me at a disadvantage. Both a stranger in this town and low on funds. However, I'm sure the agency will have a new husband for me soon."

"There's three things the West has," Maggie said. "Wide open spaces, an abundance of men, and a shortage of eligible women. You'll do just fine with finding someone. Why, by the time that letter comes, you might not even want to accept that man they offer. You might have already found one."

Alyssa laughed. "I'm not planning to look," she said. "In truth, I wasn't sure I wanted to marry, but I need stability and security urgently. Something I don't feel capable of providing for myself."

"I expect you could, if you wanted," Maggie assured her. "You seem to be very resourceful."

Alyssa flushed at the compliment. "Thank you," she said. "I just hope I can keep busy while I am here."

"Oh!" Maggie said and jumped up. "Dinner is on the stove. I'd best get busy myself. It will be ready in about an hour."

The hour passed by quickly. Alyssa had moved herself to the crackling fire in a large fireplace and let herself become drowsily hypnotized by the dancing flames. Her travel hadn't been restful. How could it be when one was shoved with a half dozen others into a small coach?

Dinner was delicious. A rich beef stew, crusty bread, and another slice of the cake she'd had earlier. Afterward,

Alyssa offered to help Maggie in her kitchen, but the older woman shook her head.

"You've had a long journey it sounds like, and then an unwelcome experience. Go rest. Who knows when you will have a chance to do that again once things settle?"

"I guess that's true," Alyssa said. "I'm just not used to sitting and doing nothing."

"There is a shelf with books near the fireplace. You are welcome to read whatever you like," Maggie said, and then she disappeared.

Alyssa roamed the café's main room. She first looked out the large windows at the street. There weren't too many people wandering around. She supposed the children were home from school, and the adults were going about their evening tasks. A wagon rode past and she looked at it hopefully. Perhaps it was the mail wagon?

When it didn't slow or stop by the post office, she turned away, feeling disappointed. Alyssa crossed to the fireplace, looked at the colorful book spines, and ran a finger longingly over the covers. She wished she could read them. Maybe that one Peter had been reading was on the shelf.

With a sigh, Alyssa turned away. She went to her room, rummaged through her bag, and then returned downstairs, a sketchbook and her pencils in hand. Sitting near the window, Alyssa lost herself in her drawing.

First, she made simple lines and shapes, then filled them in. About an hour later, Maggie wandered past and gasped as she saw the sketchbook.

"My word!" Maggie exclaimed. "Is that our town?"

"It is," Alyssa told her. "At least, what I can see from the window."

"It's wonderful," Maggie said. "It looks so realistic."

Alyssa blushed. "I enjoy drawing," she said.

"I won't bother you then," Maggie said. "If you need me, just call. I'll be in the kitchen."

With a nod, Alyssa returned to her drawing. A few more details would finish it completely. Then, perhaps tomorrow, she'd go down to the stream and sketch it as well. Maggie might pack her a small meal to take if she asked.

A short while later, Alyssa retired to her room with a tray Maggie had given her with a teapot, teacup, and a few cookies loaded onto it.

Alyssa undressed and took out her nightgown. Then she stood on tiptoe to see as much of her torso as she could in the small mirror. Even though she was glad she wasn't marrying that horrid man, Mr. Gerald Weatherbee, his words echoed around and around in her head. Shame filled her at being deemed too flat-chested to catch a man's attention. What was most painful was it was a man like that who had a complaint! She was so meager on top that she couldn't even catch *his* eye?

Angrily, Alyssa poured herself the tea with shaking hands. There was nothing wrong with her, she thought. There had never been complaints before. The problem must be him.

Still, it was going to be difficult to find a man who would take her as a bride. What with her...inability, and all. Alyssa bit her lip. It wasn't entirely her fault. There were others who also shared that... challenge. But, at the end of the day, it didn't matter, did it? Not if she wasn't good enough with her other attributes to get a husband. She had other abilities, such as being able to do a little sewing and cooking and cleaning. She was a hard worker, and willing to learn what she didn't know.

But was that enough?

A sudden worry sprang to her mind. She'd never heard of a woman being turned away before when they were a mail-order bride. What if it happened again? If it did, what should she do? Surely, the agency would think it was a fault with her. What then?

Desperation filled her. She must come up with a plan. An idea of what she could do if that happened. Taking a deep breath, Alyssa shook her head. This moment was not the time to do that. She'd figure it out. Somehow. She always did. Things hadn't gone well for her for the last several years, but that was all going to change. Alyssa was sure of it.

First, the grandmother who'd raised her died, leaving Alyssa penniless and homeless, when a distant relative sold off the small home she'd grown up in. Then, she struggled to take in work that paid enough to provide a roof over her head. A seamstress who had hired her had taken pity on Alyssa and let her sleep in her shop's back room, but she had to leave when the seamstress needed to offer that place for a family member.

It was around that same time that the mail-order bride agency had opened. Curious, Alyssa had gone there to see what everyone had been talking about. Once there, she had signed up almost immediately. The woman in charge had explained that women traveled West, got married, and their husband paid for all of their travel expenses and promised to give them a good home and treat them well, just in exchange for marrying them. Most of the men were simply lonely, the woman had said. They wanted a wife to cook and keep house, to be a companion and perhaps fall in love with.

It had seemed almost too good to be true; someone willing to protect and provide, just in trade for her cooking and cleaning? But several women had signed up ahead of her, each of them with the story of a friend or family member who'd had a successful mail-order marriage. It was enough to make Alyssa excited and hopeful.

Of course, she didn't quite have the experience she'd hoped for, but perhaps there was still time to rectify that.

Alyssa curled into the bed and angled herself to see the night sky through the window. The woman that Peter had told her about, Ophelia, haunted her thoughts. It was only now she let herself think more about her. She couldn't imagine being so in love with a man she'd kill herself over him. There had to be much more to the story.

Perhaps she could find Peter, ask about her letter, and hear more of the story. As she drifted off to sleep, Alyssa smiled. Peter had very nice eyes. The way he'd shown such concern about her, thinking she was going to fall into the water...that was just the sort of husband she hoped for. Someone who would want to protect her and treat her well. Whoever was attached to Peter was incredibly lucky.

Chapter 4

Peter had trouble sleeping. He wasn't sure if it was the fact his mind had been consumed with Miss Moore, or Alyssa as she'd invited him to call her, or if it was guilt over his thought to postpone her letter for a day or two. After hours of worrying, he'd gotten up from his bed, walked down the stairs to the post office, and checked to be sure he really had placed her letter into the mail sack.

No matter how much he wanted to do the selfish thing, to have an excuse to keep her in town a little longer, he couldn't. It wasn't who he was.

Now, however, he thought as he handed over the sack to the mail rider, he wished he hadn't put it in there.

As the rider drove off, Peter returned to the post office, holding the small sack of letters meant for Deepwater. As he set it on the counter, an envelope on the floor caught his eye. When he bent over to pick it up, he gasped.

It was the letter from Alyssa! Peter couldn't help it. He grinned, looked upward, and said, "Thank you."

While it was true, he wasn't sure if this was divine intervention or just a simple coincidence, the fact of the matter was the letter would be in his possession for three more days. His heart sped up. Now he had just a little more time with Alyssa, perhaps, and that made him excited. Not hopeful, she'd never want a man like him, but he was excited all the same.

From all the books he'd read, he'd formed the ideal woman. She would be fiery, funny, beautiful with dark hair, clever, and kind. Just in his short time with her, he was sure Alyssa was all of those things, and more.

Peter gazed across the street from the post office's front window. He could see a figure sitting in the café. Was that her? He wanted to get closer to see, but was bound to stay there, doing his duty, until lunchtime.

Minutes dragged on. The figure didn't move. It had to be her. Being new to the town, she wouldn't want to venture out far on her own, of that he felt sure. Perhaps she was reading one of the books the café had. Or lingering over tea.

At last, the appointed time came, and Peter hurriedly put up the sign letting anyone who stopped by know he'd be back in a half hour.

Peter walked across the street, trying to move slowly so his limp wasn't as obvious. It had been cold this morning, and his hip was aching. He'd rubbed some ointment on it from the doctor, but nothing really helped. A man came from the other direction with his wife. Peter looked on slightly envious.

He knew he shouldn't feel that way, but he wondered what it would be like to be someone else. Someone who walked straight without pain. Someone who had a wife who loved him.

He hesitated outside of the café door. Alyssa was inside, sitting right where he'd thought. The figure *had* been her. He felt nervous then. Would he look like a fool stopping over to see her? But this was the café. He could simply pretend he was getting something for lunch, and saw her by happenstance.

The plan appealed to him, and Peter pushed open the door. The small bell over the café door chimed as he walked in, but Alyssa didn't look up. She focused on a notebook of some sort. Peter took a moment to admire her. Her dark hair was pulled back, but an unruly piece near the front fell to her cheek. He wished he were brave enough to reach out and push it backward, letting his fingers brush against her cheek. He was sure her skin was as smooth as silk. However, he wasn't brave enough, and would have to settle for just admiring her from a distance.

Maggie came from the kitchen just then and smiled at him.

"Hello, Peter! Lunch here today?"

"Please, Maggie," he answered. "Whatever you've got is fine with me." He stepped closer to her and then winced.

She gave him a sympathetic look. "Your leg hurting?"

"It is," he shrugged. "Doc said not much he can do to help. Just one of those things."

Maggie nodded, then squeezed his hand. "Don't you worry. We've all got something."

Peter was sure she was right. After all, every book he read, someone did have something. Maybe they were poor or an orphan. Still, each, for the most part, not like in *War and Peace,* had a happy ending. The thought made him feel slightly better. Perhaps his story would also have one.

"I'll be right back," Maggie said, and turned away.

As she left, Peter glanced again at Alyssa. She hadn't been disturbed at all by the conversation. Curious as to what had captured her attention, he decided to walk over and see.

There was a book of some kind in front of her, and she was writing—no, sketching in it. Before his eyes, details of the nearby buildings nearly sprang from the page.

"Hello," Peter said, approaching.

Alyssa raised her head. "Hello," she greeted Peter with a smile.

He let out a low whistle. "That's some picture you made," he said. "Boy, that's really good."

"Do you think so?" Alyssa asked. She looked at the drawing critically. "Maggie liked it as well. I'm not much of an artist, but I do enjoy drawing. I thought I might give it to her once I'm finished. The majority was done last night. I'm just putting the final details on now."

"She'd like that," Peter assured her. "You are really talented."

"Thank you," Alyssa said, her cheeks turning pink. She toyed with the pencil, and said quietly, "I like to paint too. But I couldn't bring my supplies with me. Wherever I go to next and stay, I hope to buy more." She was quiet then, and added worriedly, "Hopefully, I will have a husband who allows that."

Peter wanted to burst out his request to marry him. To stay there. Just as quickly, he asked himself how it was possible that he'd fallen in love so quickly. She didn't feel the same. There was just no way that she did. Heck, he hardly knew her.

Just...there was this feeling of rightness. He couldn't explain it. It was like something out of a book. Love at first sight, they called it. Peter held back his sigh. Instead, he answered, "I hope you get all that you are hoping for. You deserve that."

She looked startled, but there was also a look of gratitude in Alyssa's eyes. "Thank you," she told him, and then she smiled. "The woman you have is very lucky to have someone so kind as you."

As her lips curved upward, it was as though the sun had come out from behind the clouds. Peter felt his heart palpitate with a fury that made him feel lightheaded. He grabbed on to the edge of the chair for support.

Then he realized what she'd said, and he stammered, "O-oh. I—I don't have a woman."

"I'm sure you will one day," she said, still with her beautiful smile. "And she will be very lucky."

Peter's cheeks burned. He didn't know how to answer. His stomach was flipping around, his heart was thudding, and his legs felt shaky. How was it she affected him so? She spoke again, and he forced himself to listen to her, and ignore the strange things his body was doing.

"I know it's likely too soon to know," Alyssa said, biting her lip. "But do you know when my letter will get to its destination? I'm sure they will reply quickly. But," she lowered her head, "as I'd mentioned before, I don't have much in the way of funds. I am feeling desperate, and despite my best efforts, find myself completely unable to do anything more than worry."

She laughed softly. "It seems that my plan to become a mail-order bride didn't work out, and now I must form another."

"It might take a few days to get there," Peter said. "Sometimes our mail is a little slow. Seeing as your unusual circumstances though, I'm sure that you are feeling concerned. Don't worry, anyone here in town will help you if you need it, and I'm sure you will get a reply soon."

Just then, Maggie walked up. "That's right. Don't you worry about paying me a cent, either. I suspect that mail-order bride agency will cover your expenses. If they don't, and you are still short, again, no need to worry. The church has funds they use for things like this. You wouldn't be the first stranded traveler. We'll take care of you."

Before Alyssa could open her mouth, Maggie asked, "You eating here, Peter?"

He said, "I better not."

"Oh please," Alyssa said. She looked up at him then, and that same strand of hair he longed to brush from her cheek was there. "Don't leave on my account. I'd love the company, if you've time."

"If you are sure?" he asked.

When she nodded, Maggie said, "I'll grab you a bite too, dear," and left. She returned less than a minute later with food for them both, then left, humming to herself.

"I was hoping to see you again," Alyssa said, as she picked up her fork.

His stomach jolted. She had? His chest felt tight. "Oh?" was what he said instead.

"Yes. That story, Ophelia. Did I say that right?" When he nodded, she continued, "You had said the man who was cruel to her was a prince. Did I remember that correctly?"

"Yes," Peter answered after he swallowed a bite of chicken dumplings. Maggie had spooned them and their rich gravy overtop a bed of mashed potatoes. She was one of the finest cooks he knew.

"Why did he treat her that way?" Alyssa took a bite, and watched him with a curious expression.

"Well," Peter said with a frown as he thought about the question. "It depends on who you ask. Some people have different opinions on that, even though they've read the same story."

"What is yours?" Alyssa asked.

Peter set his mug down. "Hamlet was upset at his mother. He felt betrayed by her. Then, he found out that Ophelia was asked by her father to spy on him. He was also arrogant and filled with self pity. He acted rashly, and didn't care for anyone but himself and his own feelings. He wasn't deserving of the love Ophelia had for him."

"And what was she like?" Alyssa asked.

Peter was enjoying her questions. He couldn't recall the last time he'd been able to share an interest in a book with someone. After his next bite, he answered, "She was an obedient daughter. She tried to please and make others happy. Ultimately, she discovered she couldn't make everyone happy." Then he frowned. "Or perhaps she didn't. Perhaps she'd already fallen into madness at that point."

"Trying to please others can do that," Alyssa said quietly. "She has my sympathy."

"I'm happy to loan you my book if you'd like," Peter offered. "I can bring it over this evening."

"Ahh, no, that's fine. I wouldn't want to have something so valuable."

"It's no problem," Peter assured her. Just then, he glanced over toward the post office. There was a customer waiting.

"I've got to go," Peter said. He stood and apologized, "Time got away from me."

"It was nice to have lunch with you," Alyssa said.

"Would ah...would you care to go to the church picnic with me? It's in two days," Peter said. He scuffed his toe on the ground, sure she'd say no.

"I'd be delighted," Alyssa said. "Will you come for me?"

He could hardly believe it. She had said yes. Peter felt his heart hammering again. "Y-yes. A-around eleven," he said.

As he hurried away, he didn't pay much attention to the limp or the ache in his hip. He not only had lunch and a conversation he enjoyed with Alyssa, but he was taking her to the church picnic. Him. Of all the people in the town, *he* would be the one with the beautiful woman on his arm.

Unlocking the post office door and greeting his customer, Peter wished with all his heart that the reply to Alyssa's letter wouldn't come anytime soon.

Chapter 5

Alyssa bit her lip as she looked down at her dress. She felt a little embarrassed, wondering if she was dressed appropriately, and if Peter would like what she had on. While it wasn't like she had a large variety of clothing with her, she did want to look nice. Both for the picnic and for Peter.

And she couldn't help but wonder why it concerned her so. Peter had been swimming in her mind for the last two days. That was also strange. She'd only just met him, so why did she find herself thinking about him frequently?

It was simply because he was good conversation, she told herself firmly as she pinned up her hair. Nothing more.

Not at all that there was something sweet and kind and comfortable about his ways.

But there was. A tiny voice whispered it in her ear each time she saw him or thought about him. It filled Alyssa with a wistfulness. If only she could tell Peter how she felt. But he wouldn't feel the same. Of that, she was sure. He was nothing more than kind. A friend.

It also filled her with a longing that whoever she might be sent next to marry would also possess some of those gentle ways about him. She desperately wanted someone kind, who was concerned for her. Who treated her as though she were all of the things Peter made her feel—interesting, talented, clever, beautiful.

She wasn't really any of those things. Sure, she could draw well enough, she supposed. That was about it, though. Her cooking skills were limited, but she wasn't horrible to look at, though perhaps, she thought, staring critically into the mirror, her face was a little too sharp. That might be life's circumstances though. They'd been difficult as of late.

She sighed softly and ran her hands down her front. Her dress was a medium blue, with just a touch of lace on the cuffs. Not too fancy, but not plain. She turned from the mirror with a groan. Why was she so worried? It was simply a picnic with a friend.

Alyssa left her room, closing the door gently behind her. Just as she got to the bottom of the steps, Maggie appeared from the kitchen, her hands full.

"Let me help you," Alyssa said, taking one of the pies from the other woman's hand.

"Thank you. Just place it there." Maggie nodded toward the counter, where two other pies sat.

Alyssa placed it down. "These smell wonderful," she said.

"Two beef pies and two apple pies," Maggie said with a nod. "Everyone brings plenty. There's always quite a bit left over."

"I feel bad going, and not having anything to bring," Alyssa said, biting her lip nervously.

"Oh, don't! You are staying here, and I've provided for us all," Maggie clucked. "However, in payment, you and Peter must help carry. Hank will grab one and I will take the other."

Alyssa nodded, and smiled her thanks, just as the small bell over the door chimed and Peter entered.

Her breath caught. Alyssa wasn't sure why, but it was obvious that Peter had also taken care with his appearance. He was wearing a gray shirt tucked into his dark pants, with his hair neatly combed. His black shoes were shined a glossy sheen, and he looked—nervous. Handsome, but nervous as well. That, somehow, made her relax.

"Hello," he greeted her with a smile. Then he turned to Maggie. "Can I help? I already took over the jugs of apple tea I brewed."

"Yes. You each take a pie. I'm just waiting for Hank to finish getting ready. Go ahead and start over there," Maggie said. "I'll hold the door."

A few seconds later, Alyssa and Peter were out on the sidewalk, walking toward the church. "It's a fine day for a picnic," Alyssa said. She turned her face up to the sky. "It's simply beautiful weather."

"It sure is," Peter said. She didn't miss the quick glance he shot her. "And I appreciate the good company too."

She smiled in reply, but it quickly turned into a frown as two teenagers raced past them, calling, "Clumsy Postmaster Peter! Don't drop the pies!"

"What—"

Peter's hand on her arm stopped the words about to come out of Alyssa's mouth. She turned to him. He had a smile, but his eyes were sad.

"Just ignore them," he said, and gave a little shrug.

"Ignore them? That was horrid of them. Why would they say such a thing?"

He hesitated, pausing his step, then resumed. Alyssa looked down then and noticed his limp. Had he still not healed from whatever had ailed him?

"Should we slow?" Alyssa asked him, concern in her voice. "You seem to be limping still, from however you injured yourself."

Peter flushed and looked away for a moment. She worried she'd embarrassed or upset him, but he flashed her a grin and that half shrug he seemed to do whenever he was feeling uncomfortable. "No injury," he said. "That's just me. I've got a limp and walk funny."

"Oh! I'm so sorry, I didn't mean—"

"Don't be," Peter interrupted her. "I'm used to it. Though," he added, nodding toward the way the teenagers had vanished, "that doesn't stop small minded folks from making comments every now and again."

"Does it...does it bother you?" Alyssa asked softly.

Ahead of them, a short distance away, she could see the church rising up. Its grounds were filled with blankets, chairs, and tables, with many people milling about.

"My leg?" Peter asked. "Or my feelings?"

"Both," she said. She stopped, and when he also paused, she met his gaze.

Peter locked eyes with her, and for a dizzying moment, it was as though nothing else existed but the two of them. Everything stopped, and Alyssa felt her heart beating in a strange way.

His voice broke the spell. "My leg doesn't hurt so much as my hip. From being uneven. My feelings...well, I try not to let it bother me, but words can be more painful than a physical wound."

The dreaded words about her own bosom returned to her ears, and Alyssa nodded. "I understand. I know I'm virtually a stranger, so my opinion might not matter, but I...I rather like you. I think you are a good person."

The tips of his ears turned pink, and Peter grinned at her. "Then I've all I need," he said, and continued on.

They walked the rest of the short distance in silence, but were greeted right away after stepping onto church grounds by the reverend and his wife.

"Hello and welcome to Deepwater," the reverend said, shaking her hand after she'd set down the pie. "I'm Gabriel Sullivan, and this is my wife, Laura. She's also the town's teacher."

"It's wonderful to meet you," Alyssa said. "Everyone I've had the pleasure of meeting has been so kind and welcoming to me."

The words weren't exactly a lie. She didn't consider Mr. Gerald Weatherbee or those rude teenagers people she'd met—not exactly.

"It's lovely to have a visitor to our little town," Laura said. "I do hope you will join me for tea. It's always nice to meet someone new and hear things I've not heard before. I'll send a note around to the café soon."

"I'd like that," Alyssa said, instantly liking the reverend's wife. She was so vibrant and friendly. It made her hope that she wouldn't leave too soon. She'd like to become friends with her.

"Good, we'll get together soon, I promise," Laura said.

As she and Gabriel turned to greet a family, Peter led Alyssa over to makeshift tables heaped with food.

"My goodness," Alyssa said, her eyes wide as she took it all in. "Maggie was quite right about there being plenty."

"Everyone is invited, able to bring something or not," Peter told her as he handed her a plate. "If people choose to take their leftovers, they do. But a good number actually leave them and the reverend and his wife take them to a few people on the outskirts of town who are in need and might be too shy to stop by."

"That's so thoughtful," Alyssa said, and surveyed the options in front of her. "Gracious, there's just so much. I don't know what to choose."

"Allow me to make suggestions," Peter grinned, and soon Alyssa's plate was filled with a slice of Maggie's beef pie, roasted vegetables, cornbread, mashed potatoes, fried chicken, a flaky biscuit, and a wedge of cheese.

"Just wait until they bring out the desserts," he told her as they made their way to an unattended blanket and sat.

"If I make it," she laughed.

"Oh, you will. You won't want to miss those, that's for sure," Peter said with a grin as he patted his stomach.

The reverend said a blessing and everyone ate. Alyssa took several bites, tasting everything once, then shook her head. "It's all wonderful. I'm so glad you told me what to choose."

Peter flushed again. "I'll help at dessert too," he promised.

They ate in silence, and Alyssa enjoyed the quiet companionship. With Peter, she didn't feel the need to fill in gaps of silence. It let her relax, fully, in a way she hadn't since her grandmother had passed away. Other couples, families, and groups were spread out, laughing and talking. Everyone seemed to be having a wonderful time. She was so glad she'd come. This was much nicer than staying alone at the café, like she'd considered this morning.

"Thank you for inviting me," Alyssa said. Then she reached for her handbag. "I have something for you."

"You do?" Peter looked surprised.

"Yes." Alyssa carefully withdrew the rolled-up piece of paper, relieved to see it hadn't been damaged. She handed it to Peter, hesitated, then said, "That is, if you'd like it."

Peter tugged on the scrap of twine Maggie had given her to tie around the paper, and then unrolled her surprise slowly. He sucked in his breath. "That's the stream. Where we met."

"Where you almost pushed me in," Alyssa laughed.

"Where I rescued you," he retorted with a laugh of his own.

"Perspectives vary," Alyssa said, giggling. "But yes, I went there yesterday and drew this. I wanted you to have it."

Peter hadn't taken his eyes off the gift. He was quiet as he studied it, then said, "I will treasure it always. No one has ever given me anything so special."

"It's just a drawing," Alyssa said, ducking her head as her cheeks drew warm.

"It's more than that," Peter said, his serious eyes meeting hers. "It was your time, and effort, and that you were thinking of me."

Alyssa caught her breath. When he said it like that, it almost felt...romantic. Her cheeks turned even hotter.

"I brought my book. *Hamlet*. I...I would like you to have it. So that you can enjoy it, as much as I have." He offered her the volume, and looked at her expectantly.

There was a terrifying jolt in Alyssa's stomach. "I can't accept that," she protested.

"I want you to have it. To read," Peter insisted.

She shook her head, then looked around. It didn't appear that anyone was listening. Should she tell him? Her secret burned terribly, filling her with shame and fear. But Peter's eyes met hers, and she felt a strange comfort. Reassurance as he reached for her hand.

"Is something wrong?" he asked quietly. "You can tell me. I didn't offend you, did I?"

"Oh no," Alyssa gasped. "It wasn't that at all." She bit her lip. "It's just...you see...I..."

How was she going to admit this? Peter was so intelligent, surely he'd look down on her. She took a deep breath, and drew comfort from his warm hand wrapped around hers.

Looking up and into his eyes, Alyssa whispered, "I can't read."

Chapter 6

The moment Alyssa told him she couldn't read, Peter felt a surge of relief go through him. So that's why she'd refused his offer of the book. It wasn't that she didn't like him. He caught sight of her distressed look and squeezed her hands reassuringly.

"So what?" he asked.

His answer seemed to take her off guard. She blinked a few times, seemingly in shock, so Peter continued. "I can't draw. And I walk with a limp. We all have something." Maggie's words from earlier rang in his ears and he realized they were more than true.

He pointed to a woman sitting across the lawn from her. "She is deaf. Oh, and the man over there standing by the tree? One hand. If you were to look around at each of the people here, every single one of them has something about them that they don't like or gives them trouble or a challenge from time to time."

She still looked confused, so Peter continued to point, though discreetly. "Brown hair, blue eyes, blonde hair, green eyes, lefthanded or right, we all have something different about us."

"I think I understand what you are saying," Alyssa said. She shook her head then. "But...I can't read. And you do. Doesn't that bother you? That I am not as educated as you are?"

"Oh, I'm not the least bit educated," Peter said, shaking his head. "It's a long story. Well read, yes. Educated, no. But to answer your question, it doesn't bother me at all. Why would it?" He grinned then. "What it does do, is give me an opportunity."

"An opportunity?"

"Yes." Peter jumped up and reached for her hand. "Dessert is out. Let's get some and I'll explain."

Like before, Alyssa listened to his suggestions, and soon they walked back to their blanket, with oatmeal cookies, Maggie's apple pie, and a wedge of chocolate cake, covered in a rich frosting.

They resumed their spots on the blanket and took a few bites. Alyssa asked, "So, what did you mean by, I had an opportunity?"

Peter looked up and met her eyes. Then he sucked in his breath. She was so beautiful. He could hardly believe that she was here with him. Her eyes pulled him in deeply, and he wished for nothing more than to be like this forever, sitting here with her, her eyes locked onto his, and her comfortable presence close by.

When Alyssa moved slightly, it shook him from the trance he'd been in. "Ah, yes." He cleared his throat, trying to regain his thoughts. After they were in some form of coherence, he said, "While you wait for your letter, you've got some time to learn how to read. I can teach you. There's nothing to it. Really, once you learn the basics of what letters work together and the sounds they make, you'll pick it right up and be able to continue on your own when you do leave."

As painful as it was to add those last words, Peter knew she would one day. But if he taught her to read, well, a small piece of him would always be with her. He liked that idea. Before she left, he was determined to give her his copy of *Hamlet* as well. To remember him by.

Her face was one of hesitation. "Aren't I too old?"

"No, we'll start simple. I can come to the café when the post office closes and we can work for an hour or so there or by the stream or at one of the café tables if you like." Peter waited to see what she'd decide. Alyssa had a thoughtful look on her face. Then, she smiled and it lit up her whole face.

"I'd love to. Thank you, Peter."

A shiver went through him, and he masked it by reaching for another bite.

As the picnic wound down, Peter walked Alyssa back to the café. They went slowly, almost as if each of them wasn't ready for their time to end.

Peter led her by the stream, then touched his pocket where he'd placed the drawing she'd given him. He'd treasure that forever, and hang it up where he could look at it every day.

The water trickled over the stones, and they smiled at each other, Alyssa letting out a little giggle at the exact spot where they'd first met. How foolish he'd been that day. However, Peter reflected, had he not acted before thinking, he'd have never gotten to meet Alyssa, nor had such a wonderful day like he did today.

Alongside the bank, small wildflowers in a lavender color popped up and Peter plucked one. He felt nervous, but wouldn't let himself think. He would only act. Thinking would make him too scared to offer it to Alyssa.

He held the flower toward her, and tried not to feel nervous as he said, "A reminder of today."

Alyssa took the flower, her fingers brushing his as she accepted it, then held it to her face. "Thank you, Peter," she said, giving him that smile that he'd now do anything for. "I promise you, I'll never forget today, not as long as I live."

They continued on in silence, slowly meandering back through the town. Peter wasn't sure if she was walking slower because of his limp or because she didn't want to return, but he sure hoped it was the latter.

Arriving far too soon to his liking at the café's door, she reached out and squeezed his hand gently. He thought his chest might burst, his heart swelled up so full.

"Thank you," Alyssa said softly, then released his hand, giving him one more of those radiant smiles.

She went inside and he returned slowly to his home, her words from earlier playing in his mind.

"I know I'm virtually a stranger, so my opinion might not matter, but I...I rather like you. I think you are a good person."

She had been so genuine. And just a moment ago, when she'd reached for his hand? Peter had never felt so happy.

And guilty.

He'd have to make sure that letter of hers was in the next mail. How could he be a man worthy of another's love when he did something that could be thought of as deceitful?

Chapter 7

The next morning, Alyssa sat in the café's dining room and waited for Maggie to bring her breakfast. Again, she'd offered to help, but again, Maggie had said no.

When a tray came out a few moments later, loaded with apple cider, warm cornbread drizzled with honey, oats, and an apple with a wedge of cheese, she started to tuck in, then stopped.

"Thank you. Everyone here has been so kind to me. You most of all." Alyssa smiled. "I will miss you when I am gone."

"We should write," Maggie offered.

"I'm going to learn how," Alyssa said. She admitted, "I don't know how to read or write—yet. Peter has offered to teach me."

"Ah, he's a good man. Our town wouldn't be the same without him," Maggie nodded.

Alyssa nodded in agreement. Last night, she'd pressed the small flower he'd given her between some pages in her sketchbook. For as long as she lived, she'd keep it. It would be a precious reminder of him and of their day together.

Then a memory returned, and her brow furrowed. "Something terrible happened yesterday," Alyssa said. "It didn't seem to upset Peter, but it did me."

"What's that?" Maggie asked, sitting herself down across from Alyssa.

"We were on our way to the church when several teenagers ran past and started teasing him because of how he walked." Alyssa bit her lip. "I was going to say something, but I got the feeling he didn't want me to."

"Yes," Maggie said, her eyes darkening. "A few young ones don't understand the hard lives others have had. Some folks, through no fault of their own."

"What happened to his leg?" Alyssa asked. "If I might be allowed to know? I hope that doesn't seem rude of a question."

"Not at all," Maggie said. "I don't know the full story, but it was something that happened in his youth." She shook her head then, "We've all got something though, and no one should make fun of another."

"That's similar to what Peter said," Alyssa mused, "when I told him my shameful secret."

"You've a shameful secret?" Maggie eyed her up and down critically. "You might think so, but I doubt it."

"It's true," Alyssa said, and looked away briefly. Once she'd gathered her courage, she admitted, "My not being able to read is shameful. I know Peter has said he's going to teach me, but do you...do you think he can?"

"I suspect so," Maggie said, and reached over to pat her hand. "Lots of folks can't read, but I know plenty who have learned later in life."

"Really?" Maggie's words and nonchalant expression made Alyssa feel hopeful. A small part of her that she hadn't known was tense relaxed. "That makes me feel better." She smiled then. "I'm looking forward to the first lesson, and I hope I do well."

"I am sure that won't be a problem," Maggie said with a smile. "You're a clever girl, and anyone who can draw the way you do will very easily pick up something like reading."

Maggie got a curious look on her face. "Do you mind if I ask how it came to be that you never learned?"

"Not at all." Shaking her head, Alyssa said, "It wasn't a priority for my parents. In fact, I don't even recall going to school until I was a little older and moved in with my grandmother. By that point, teachers assumed I could read, and I learned little tricks to avoid doing so. I could copy beautifully, even if I didn't know just what I was writing, so that's what I did, feigning I was too shy or had a sore throat. With other students misbehaving, as I was so quiet I was quite overlooked."

"Harumph," Maggie said. "A shame. They didn't do you right. But never you mind. I suspect Peter will teach you quickly."

"When I do learn," Alyssa said, "I am going to read every book I can get my hands on." She felt excited at the thought. She wouldn't have to ask others to tell her about what they were reading and wonder how it ended. Every bit of that knowledge would be hers, and she hungered for it, far more than she ever thought she would.

For years, Alyssa had pretended that it had not mattered to her that she couldn't read, and honestly she'd gotten by just fine as her memory was quite good. However, to be able to read shop signs and packages on items? Newspapers and books? A letter that arrived for her? The possibilities were endless and she just hoped that it really wouldn't be difficult, as she didn't want to make a fool of herself.

"I can tell you are worrying a little," Maggie said, with her eyes nearly piercing through Alyssa. "You got quite excited looking, but then I saw your shoulders sag."

Alyssa smiled. She couldn't help it. Being around Maggie made her feel happy. The woman had such an easy manner about her. "You seem to read people well," she said, then confessed, "I'm a little worried. About reading, about having enough time to learn to read. Maggie, I find myself in a little bit of a problem.

"You see, as anxious as I am to find out where I'm meant to be in my future, I find that I'm not in a hurry to leave here. I'm rather enjoying Deepwater and most of the people in the town. I feel at home, which is rather an odd thing to feel, living in a room at a café, with only a bag to my name, and having been rejected as a mail-order bride."

Maggie was quiet a moment, then nodded. "I understand that feeling. Deepwater has a way of finding and keeping folks if they are meant to be here."

"How so?" Alyssa asked.

"More than a few of us never intended to settle here in Deepwater, but," Maggie shrugged, "here we are. Myself and my husband, our wagon broke down. The reverend wasn't originally from here either, but felt the call. His wife was actually traveling on a stagecoach on her way to be a teacher somewhere else when the stage broke down and she was trapped here."

Maggie leaned back and crossed her arms, her grin wide. "You'd never know it, but she and the reverend saved the town from highwaymen. They also saved me, when one had me tied up."

"What?" Alyssa gasped.

Waving her hand, Maggie shrugged. "That's another story for another day. But yes, if you are meant to be here, I think things will work out so you can be. After all, look at you now. Perhaps things are already going as they should be."

She turned toward the kitchen without another word, and Alyssa frowned. That was a point to ponder. Was what she suggested true? Had things already been set into motion and planned out how they should be? She couldn't understand how her feelings being hurt—not to mention the complete humiliation at her rejection—was a good thing, but perhaps there was a little truth to this. After all, most everyone else in Deepwater had been pleasant. She knew when the time came, she'd miss Maggie and Peter. She also wanted to get to know Laura better.

Alyssa couldn't remember ever having friends of her own or people she could talk to so easily. It wasn't a feeling that she was anxious to give up, not after she'd just gotten it.

Suddenly, Alyssa felt incredibly sad. Picking up her spoon, she ate her breakfast, hoping it might provide a distraction. If only she could slow time. Make sure that she had all she needed. Time here, in Deepwater. Time to learn to read and write. Time to be with Peter.

Her hand stilled, a spoonful of oatmeal half to her lips. Time with Peter? Where had that come from?

But even as she questioned the thought, she knew that was something that she did actually want. Not just with him as a teacher, but as a friend. She half wondered if he'd ever want something more.

But that was foolish. Not with a woman like her. She wasn't nearly as intelligent as him, and he deserved so much better.

Better to remember that, before being rejected again.

Chapter 8

Peter slowly got dressed. Then he slowly made his breakfast. Afterward, he slowly opened the door to the post office. He wasn't sure what was wrong with him, but he just wasn't feeling himself. He felt sluggish.

It didn't make sense, either. Today, he was supposed to give Alyssa her first reading lesson. Shouldn't he be excited to spend time with her? That was what he wanted, wasn't it?

As his eyes fell on the sack of letters ready to go on today's mail wagon, a sudden understanding washed over him. He knew exactly what was wrong. Today, he'd be getting a mail delivery. That meant Alyssa might be getting a letter. A letter that might take her away from him.

A sick feeling washed over him, but at least he could be assured that this wasn't the kind of illness he needed to see a doctor for. Honestly, what he was feeling, alongside of the sadness and feeling of impending doom, was just a tad bit of guilt.

He toed the sack of letters. Hers had gone out. He'd made sure of it. But he hadn't liked it. If she got a letter today, what would he do? Could he really let himself forget it had arrived? Perhaps lay it somewhere and forget all about it?

No.

No, for as much as he wanted to keep Alyssa here and with him, Peter knew he had to be honest. The guilt weighing on him at his consideration of not giving her a letter if it arrived made him feel sick, though. He wished there was a way to relieve himself of the terrible thought and the guilt filling him.

Just then, the door opened. Peter looked up. As the reverend walked in, a bright sunbeam rose above his head. Peter's jaw dropped, and his eyes widened. Was this...a sign from God? Was he supposed to confess what he'd done?

Peter swallowed hard. He wasn't sure. Then he realized Gabriel was staring at him.

"You alright, Peter?" the reverend asked.

"Yes, yes, just fine," Peter stammered. "Mail's not here yet."

"That's fine. I've one to send out," Gabriel said, reaching into his jacket pocket. "It's for Laura."

"I'll see it gets sent," Peter promised, and dropped the letter into the mail sack.

"I'm glad you brought Miss Moore to the picnic," Gabriel said, leaning against the counter. "She seems quite nice. Laura is looking forward to having her over for tea."

"She'll enjoy that, I'm sure," Peter said.

He was also thinking, hoping, that if Alyssa and Laura became friends, it would be even harder for her to leave.

That wave of guilt washed over him again, and before Peter even realized he was doing it, he blurted, "I think I've sinned."

Gabriel looked surprised. "Oh?"

"Yes," Peter said. "I-I feel badly about it too. I seem to be thinking selfishly, and I can't stop feeling guilty."

"This sounds serious," Gabriel said. "Do you want to tell me what happened? Perhaps I can help to set your conscience at ease."

Peter nodded. "I think I had better," he said, his voice low. "You see, Alyssa—Miss Moore—asked me to post a letter for her. One that might take her away from here soon."

"I see. Go on," the reverend encouraged.

"Well, I...I meant to mail it. Only..."

"Only?"

"Only I didn't. Right away, I mean. I did. It went out. Just...not right away." Peter felt flustered. He realized from the ache in his leg he was pacing and stopped, sitting himself on the high stool and rubbing at his hip. "I wasn't trying to be dishonest. Really. I just...I don't know."

Gabriel was silent for a moment, the corners of his mouth twitching in a strange fashion. Then, to Peter's surprise, he gave him a gentle smile. "Do you want to know what I think?" he asked.

Peter nodded and swallowed hard.

"I think perhaps if you tell Miss Moore just what happened, she'll forgive you. I also think that if you tell Miss Moore that you are interested in her, perhaps she'll stay, and you won't need to resort to tricks to find a way to become friends with her."

The reverend's eyes were filled with amusement. Peter, however, didn't feel the same. Tensing, he pretended to be busy and shuffled some papers before he asked, "And what makes you think I'm interested in her?"

Gabriel shrugged. "I suppose that same instinct I get that she's interested in you."

Peter felt his chest tighten. Could she really be? He didn't want to dare hope it, but how he wished it were true.

"My friend," Gabriel said, leaning closer with sympathy in his voice, "you must say something sooner rather than later. The day will arrive that the answer to her letter comes. It might even be something that takes her away shortly thereafter. Don't waste this chance that you have, this moment that may never repeat itself because you are scared."

Peter wanted to object. To tell Gabriel he wasn't scared. But the truth of the matter was the scared feeling nearly consumed him. Alyssa was too perfect. Too clever, and talented, a good conversationalist, beautiful, kind...all those things that were for other men. Not a cripple like him.

Gabriel patted his shoulder. "Just think about it," he said, then turned to leave. He stopped at the door and offered, "If you need to talk more, just find me. I'm always around."

The soft closing of the door left Peter alone with his thoughts and his worries. He knew that Gabriel was right. Of course he was. It wasn't just that he was a man of God, but he was also a good friend, one who wouldn't lie. He was also someone who had nearly lost the woman he'd loved himself, by being too afraid.

Peter sighed. He checked the time, and as if he summoned it, the mail wagon pulled up. In less than a minute, the sack of outgoing mail was on its way, and the incoming mail was sitting in a sack, waiting to be sorted.

The very first letter, the one right on the top, was addressed to Alyssa.

Chapter 9

Alyssa had gone to see Peter at his lunch break to start her reading lesson, but his counter was swarming with people excited to get their letters from the day's mail. Peter looked worn out, and she saw his limp looked worse.

"I'm closing up a half hour early," he'd told her, "since I can't get away for lunch. Let's meet at four?"

She had nodded, smiling, and waved at him. "See you by the stream!" she had said.

And that's where she was headed now. Her sketchbook and pencils were tucked in a basket, along with some apples, ham sandwiches, and some freshly baked oatmeal cookies Maggie had sent along with her.

"That boy doesn't usually get a chance for lunch on mail days," Maggie had fussed. "The whole town swarms him like a pack of starving animals when they see that mail wagon."

"They must be very excited," Alyssa had said.

"Impatient is more like it," Maggie had snorted, and then sent Alyssa on her way.

The whole time that she walked, she wondered if she had also gotten a letter and what it might say. Would the mail-order bride agency ask her to return? Would they have already found someone for her, perhaps right nearby? Surely, they would let her have a say in who she married and where she went. She had before. She just hadn't known how horrible the man was until she arrived.

Alyssa shuddered. Perhaps she didn't want to be a mail-order bride after all. But what else could she do?

As she approached the stream just a little before four, Alyssa sat down and started sketching a small yellow bird at the water's edge. She was so focused on what she was doing, and trying to capture the bird before it flew away, she was startled when someone dropped next to her.

"Hello," Peter said.

"Hello," Alyssa answered, then she teased, "I wasn't sure the town would let you get away, the way they all clustered about you!"

"I wish I had someone there to help me," Peter groaned, dropping his head into his hands. "Twice a week this happens. Even folks who don't usually get letters swarm. I can hardly get the letters sorted before they find out the mail has arrived and crowd around. Many times I'm still sorting it when they rush me."

"Maggie sent me with sandwiches for us," Alyssa said, and pushed the basket toward him. "She thought you wouldn't have gotten to eat."

Peter reached inside and pulled out four wrapped sandwiches. He offered them to Alyssa, who took one. "Tell her thank you for me," he said, happily peeling back the paper. "I'm famished."

"There's apples and fresh cookies too," Alyssa said, removing them from the basket.

"She's a saint. So are you," Peter said.

They ate quietly for a few moments, until nearly all Maggie had packed was gone. Peter seemed to have something on his mind and Alyssa wondered what it was. Did he perhaps have news of a letter for her?

Alyssa hesitated. She hated to ask, both because she didn't want to bother Peter and she was worried what the answer might be, but she did, anyway.

"Peter, by chance did I..."

"Yes!" Peter patted his pockets, and then produced an envelope. "Yes, you got a letter too. I'm sorry I didn't give it to you right away. I forgot."

"There's no need to apologize," Alyssa said. She took it from him, then softly asked, "Would you mind reading it to me?"

"It would be my privilege," Peter said. He took the letter from her and then opened it slowly.

Alyssa wondered, as he pulled out the letter and paused before reading, if he was as reluctant as she was to see what it said. She might not know her words, but she knew it was a short message. There wasn't much written on the page. Sitting next to him, Alyssa leaned closely. "I wish I could make out some of this," she said, trying not to feel frustrated.

Peter put his finger under the first word. "I'll read slowly, and point to each word," he told her. "Don't worry, soon, you'll be able to read for yourself."

She shrugged, and didn't answer, too focused on where his finger was underneath the first set of squiggles she knew made up a word.

Clearing his throat, Peter read. He was true to his word, and pointed to each set of letters. "Miss Moore, we are very sorry this has happened. Please wait there in Deepwater. We will find someone else and write you soon with where to go."

Alyssa sat back. "That's it? That's all it says?"

Peter nodded. "Yes. Shall I read it again?"

Disappointment flooded Alyssa. "No, it's okay," she told him. "I had just hoped that they would have said more than just to wait."

"Let's start your lesson," Peter said. "Then, when the next letter comes, you might be able to read parts of it on your own." He handed her the letter. "Keep this, and you can practice reading it. You know this is your name, Moore," he said as he pointed to the letters, "so as you practice reading *Miss Moore*, you'll get familiar with how those words look."

Alyssa smiled. "Yes! Yes, I will," she said, suddenly feeling hopeful. "Let's start."

Peter produced a slate and pencil. "I know you said you could copy well, so let's start with letters. A," he said as he wrote it. "L. Y. S. S. A. There. That spells Alyssa."

Alyssa took the pencil from him and copied her name several times. "Alyssa," she whispered. "It looks pretty. All the curves."

"Just like you," Peter said, and as she glanced at him, she saw he was beet red. "I-I—"

But she laughed. Never had she seen anyone so flustered. Alyssa put her hand on him. She wasn't sure if he meant she had curves or that she was pretty, but it didn't matter. It made her feel happy, especially after her very unwelcome introduction to Deepwater and the men there.

A warmth spread through Alyssa, and she was very aware of Peter's hand suddenly covering hers. She looked into his eyes and saw him staring at her. She wanted to say something, though she wasn't sure what, but felt frozen to the spot. It was obvious he felt the same.

Alyssa hoped he wouldn't move his hand. In truth, she wanted him to hold both of her hands. Her chest felt tight, and just as she'd summoned enough courage to speak, there was a shriek and a splash, and children came rushing toward the stream.

As she startled, Peter did too, and pulled away, then looked at her sheepishly. "School's out," he told her.

"So I see," she agreed, her lips unable to stop the smile that formed. Feeling bold, she reached for his hand again and squeezed it. "Will we have another lesson tomorrow?"

"Yes. And I will meet you at the café at noon, then there again after. That way we shouldn't be disturbed by getting splashed." Peter stroked his thumb over her hand, and Alyssa wondered if he knew he was doing it. As soon as that thought finished, he suddenly jerked away again and got to his feet. "Walk you back?" he offered.

Feeling disappointed, Alyssa nodded. "Yes, please."

She gathered her sketchbook and pencils and wished that she could know better what Peter was thinking. She was feeling confused, and didn't like it one bit.

Chapter 10

As they started to walk away, Peter felt angry at himself. Why couldn't he tell Alyssa how he felt? He was so relieved when the letter had simply told her to wait there. That's what she'd have to do now. Was she disappointed? He thought so, but maybe he wasn't reading her well enough. He wasn't used to being around women.

Gabriel's reminder that he needed to tell her how he felt, and before it was too late, played in his mind. But he just couldn't. Whenever he felt a moment was right, it passed quickly, and he found himself frozen up with fear at saying the words that had so much potential to get him rejected. He couldn't seem to find that burst of courage like he had when he'd given her that flower after the picnic. What was wrong with him?

His heart was still pounding from a few moments before. Just before the children had gained their freedom from school, he had thought...well, it didn't matter what he'd thought or hoped. There was no way that she was going to kiss him. Not her. And there was no way that he was brave enough to try and kiss her.

Peter tried not to let his misery or his upset at himself show. He could see Alyssa's worried glances at him, and she slipped her arm through his. He liked that. Even if he didn't like how she could now feel his limp. He hated that limp. He knew others noticed it, even if they pretended not to. The pain that came with it filled him with loathing. So did how it had never healed right after the accident.

Of course, he'd never have told anyone that. Not even the reverend. It wasn't right to go around with anger or hate in your heart, even if it was directed at yourself, and he didn't want to be judged. He just wanted to stop feeling pain from his leg. No matter how he downplayed it, the ache was getting worse, and Peter feared one day he'd need a cane or a crutch. Just one more thing for people to notice.

"Pokey Peter!" a boy shouted, as he ran past, and threw a stone at him.

"Clumsy, clumpy, cripple!" another laughed, and pretended to stagger down the street.

Alyssa gasped and pulled away, taking several steps toward them. "How dare you," she said, raising her voice. "Get back here, you miscreants!"

"Just ignore it," Peter said quietly.

"I will not!" Alyssa said, nearly shouting. "They threw stones at you."

"Were you hit?" Peter asked anxiously.

"I was not their target," Alyssa said. "And I will find those children and see their parents punish them properly."

"Aye, I will," the shoemaker said, coming up then. "I'm sorry, Peter. That boy of mine, he's gotten in a bad way. Muddied his ma's laundry yesterday, blunted my awl today. I'll bring him around to make amends."

"There's no need—" Peter started

"Yes, there is," Alyssa said, her face fierce. Peter wanted to step back he was so alarmed. "If a child thinks they can get away with treating someone like that when they are a child, then what do you think happens when they grow up? They become like that horrid man I am happily not going to be wed to."

She strode down the street and Peter raced to catch up with her, with the shoemaker's apologies still going. She was muttering to herself as he took her arm again to slow her.

"Why are most of the males in this town so horrible?" She glared about her, obviously angry.

It wasn't the first time she'd said something to that effect, but she'd never explained what she meant. Hesitating, a little bit worried to upset her himself and get that glare turned onto him, Peter asked, "Most people in this town are good, and I'm disappointed that these children and the man who rejected you, foolishly, I might add, have upset you. Was there anyone else who has? Can I help you in some way to feel better?"

She stopped and took a deep breath. Her red face had turned almost white. "When I think about that man," she said, almost in a growl.

"What on earth did he say to have upset you so much?" Peter asked, alarmed. "I just assumed that it was something like he was no longer interested in a marriage."

"Oh, he was no longer interested alright," Alyssa agreed. She leaned in closely. "I've never been so humiliated in my life."

"I don't understand why he'd be that way," Peter said, bewildered. "You're the most incredible woman I've ever talked to. He must have been a real fool."

She shook her head. "I was spared, that's for sure."

"Were you too clever for him?" Peter asked, still confused and wondering just what had happened.

"No, I was...lacking in other areas," Alyssa said, as she started walking again.

"Lacking? You?" Peter stared at her in shock.

"Yes," she said, and pressed her lips tight. "In my bosom."

Peter froze. He was sure he must look a sight, because Alyssa laughed then. "Isn't that something?" she said. "It wasn't proper for me to say that to you, I'm sure, but it still shocks and upsets me. I'm quite over the hurt now. But at the time..." she shook her head and tugged on his arm. "As for making me feel better, you've done that in great quantity. I feel quite lucky to have met you, and even more happy that we are friends."

He let himself be pulled ahead, but inside, Peter was a combination of flattered and furious. He'd like to find the man and give him a piece of his mind. Lacking? Not Alyssa! Why, she filled out her bodice nicely. Not that he'd looked. It wasn't a gentlemanly thing to do. Well, not more than a peek. On accident. When he'd looked down. That was beside the point. It wasn't on purpose. Not really. But she wasn't lacking at all. Her shape was—not appropriate to think about.

Then another thought came to mind. What if the man changed his mind if he did confront him, and demand that Alyssa marry him as originally planned? Did they have some sort of a contract saying they must? The idea made him worry first, and then shudder. Her being with someone so vile repulsed him.

"We're here," Alyssa said softly.

As Peter looked up, still lost in his thoughts, Alyssa leaned forward and brushed her lips against his cheek. The tinkle of the door's bell had long faded before he took his hand off his cheek and realized he was still standing there, looking at the door she had gone through like some sort of lovesick fool. Even that slightly sobering thought didn't wipe the grin off his face as he went back home.

Chapter 11

Alyssa had hardly slept last night or the two previous nights. Her emotions were swirling around and caused her to toss and turn and stare at the ceiling. Perhaps when she had a home of her own, she'd paint a mural on the ceiling, so if there were more nights like this, she could use the moon's glow to take her mind off of whatever was worrying her, by letting her eyes focus on the painting and distract her.

This morning, shadows had been under her eyes, and she was more than grateful the water inside the pitcher in her room was so cold. It had helped a little, if by nothing else, to put some pink into her cheeks.

After dressing, Alyssa settled into the routine she'd acquired over the last few days. Breakfast and drawing, then a short lesson with Peter, a late lunch, and an evening lesson with Peter.

So far, there hadn't been another letter for her, and she wasn't entirely sure if she was making progress with her ability to recognize letters, but she was trying very hard.

Today, she was going to copy out that letter she'd received and practice reading the words. She thought that she was recognizing the shapes of some of the words better, but only time would tell. Peter assured her she was doing well, and Alyssa hoped he wasn't just saying that to be kind.

As soon as Alyssa came down the stairs, almost as if by magic, Maggie had slid her breakfast in front of her and vanished again. Today, sausages still sizzled on the plate, and there was a sweet roll and a bowl of grits waiting, along with a cup of tea.

Hungrily, Alyssa ate, then pushed the plates back and pulled out her sketchbook. She fully intended to start copying the letter, making her own letter to practice from just in case something happened to the first, but without really thinking, she started to draw instead.

Strokes and circles turned into an outline as she copied the image burned into her mind. Soon, she stared at a completed face. Alyssa startled as she realized who it was.

"That's a very good likeness of Peter," Maggie remarked, next to Alyssa's shoulder.

"I suppose I can't stop thinking about him," Alyssa said with a sigh. At Maggie's grin and raised eyebrow, she quickly added, "I wish there was a way I could help him."

"Help him?" Maggie furrowed her brow. "In what way?"

"With how the children tease him. How his leg always aches." Alyssa felt her shoulders slump. "He's so kind to others, it's not fair he should suffer so."

"I agree," Maggie said with a sigh of her own.

Just then, the café door opened, and the reverend came over to them, smiling. "Good morning," he greeted. "I come as a messenger." He offered Maggie the note, and then apologized, "I'm afraid I can't stay to talk. You ladies have a wonderful rest of your morning."

He was gone just as quickly as he came, and Maggie opened the note. "We've been invited to tea with Laura, the reverend's wife," she said with a smile.

Alyssa frowned at the note Maggie held. She wished she could understand it. Suddenly, she gasped. "Wait! Maggie!" She took the note, and then compared it to her letter from the mail-order agency. "That's my name! Alyssa."

Her heart was racing. She recognized her name. This must be a good first start. Perhaps soon she could read more words.

Maggie was smiling broadly as well. "Why, yes, it is. Those lessons you've been having are paying off."

Pride surged through Alyssa. She couldn't wait to tell Peter her news later. It was certain that he would also be proud of her.

"When do we leave?" Alyssa asked, looking for a long moment at the note before handing it back to Maggie.

"In about an hour," Maggie said. She folded the paper and handed it back to Alyssa. "Here, you keep it, dear. Perhaps some of the words on here will match words on your other letter."

Would they? Alyssa wasn't sure, but she eagerly accepted the invitation and compared the two. Now she had two notes of her own to practice and memorize. Later, she'd show Peter and get his opinion about how she could get more.

"I'll meet you back here in a little while," Maggie called as she walked away. "I'm going to get Hank to watch the counter for me."

Alyssa nodded and gathered her drawing supplies to return it to her room. She was excited to be invited. This might be the first time she'd ever had an invitation to someone's house for tea and conversation. When she'd lived with her grandmother, they kept to themselves, at her grandmother's request. She was a woman suspicious by nature, who much preferred her own company, or that of Alyssa. The only times Alyssa had ever really spoken to others was when she'd picked up supplies from the store.

As Alyssa brushed her hair, she paused. Had her grandmother known how to read? Thinking back, she didn't think so. They had no books, and when she'd once asked her about them, her grandmother had gotten very upset. If she had thought to ask the teacher, perhaps she could have learned from a primer.

The schoolhouse had several McGuffey readers, but she'd been thinking more about not wanting to be embarrassed, than thinking about how much she was missing out on and how difficult it would be later to navigate the world without that knowledge. It was easy to be taken advantage of without the ability to know something for yourself.

Still lost in her thoughts of the past, Alyssa went down the stairs and nearly bumped into Maggie, who was wrapping her shawl around her.

"There you are. Are you ready?" the other woman asked.

"Yes, I am. I'm quite excited," Alyssa confessed.

"So am I," Maggie said. "Owning your own business means that you are always tied to it, especially when there's cooking involved. One of these days, I'm going to hire someone to give me a hand."

"I'd love to help you if you need it," Alyssa said eagerly.

"I know you would, hon," Maggie said. "Can't have a guest working, though."

"If I lived here, I'd love to work at the café," Alyssa said. "It's so comfortable and cozy. I have such a good feeling whenever I am inside."

"That pleases me to no end," Maggie said, as the church came into view. "However, if you stayed, I think the post office might need you more."

Alyssa's cheeks colored.

"This way," Maggie added, saving her from answering as they walked behind the small church. "Their home is up this path."

Alyssa followed. She'd have never known there was a home behind the church. They passed a small garden with a bench, a cluster of trees, and up a well-worn path. When it opened before them, a charming little white house stood, flowers planted in it, and a smiling Laura waiting.

"Come in! I'm so glad to see you both," she said with a smile.

"Thank you for inviting me," Alyssa said shyly.

"Of course, I had to! I think that we are going to be good friends," Laura told her.

They followed Laura inside. The house was small, but comfortable and cozy. The kitchen was already set up for tea. Cups and saucers, a plate with bread and butter, another with slices of cake, and a third with cookies sat waiting.

Alyssa took her chair and listened to the reverend's wife and Maggie start talking. Laura must have sensed her still feeling shy, for she asked, "How have you enjoyed your unexpected time in our town?"

"More than I thought," Alyssa admitted. "I'm becoming very fond of it, and almost wish I could stay."

"Deepwater does that," Laura said with a knowing nod. "That's just what happened to me. I didn't want to even be here when my stage broke down just before Christmas. But then...well, I didn't want to leave."

"Alyssa's gotten one letter from the mail-order agency," Maggie explained. "It just told her to wait, though. No resolution to her situation."

"Oh dear." Laura looked at her sympathetically. "That must be stressful."

"In a way it is," Alyssa admitted. "The thing I worry the most about is providing for my needs. My money isn't unlimited, and the agency didn't send me any."

"You must not worry about that," Laura said immediately. "You will be helped if you need it. We have a town fund for that."

"For a stranger?" Alyssa couldn't help but keep the surprise from her voice.

"You used to be a stranger," Laura said with a smile and she poured the tea. "But now, you are a friend."

Sure she looked flustered at the kindness, Alyssa raised her cup to her lips and sipped the tea to hide her emotion. It was lovely. Cloves, lemon, mint, and something else. She took another sip and set her cup down.

"Do help yourselves," Laura said, gesturing to the plates.

Maggie did, then Alyssa did too. As Laura was reaching to pour more tea, the table shook slightly.

"Ugh, this wobbly leg," Laura said. "One is a bit short." She knelt down and Alyssa peered under the table to watch. "If I just put something under the short leg, like this thin piece of wood, it doesn't feel crooked anymore when pressure is put on it."

Alyssa froze. Slowly, she straightened, her mind spinning frantically. Her eyes got very wide.

"Are you alright?" Maggie asked, concerned.

"Yes. More than alright. I think—I think I know how to help Peter walk better," Alyssa whispered.

Chapter 12

Peter yawned. He was tired. Alyssa would never know, but after their evening lessons, he hurried back to the post office to get caught up on work he'd usually do earlier in the day. However, he'd rather work late into the night and be tired than miss a moment with her. Who knows how long she'd be there in Deepwater?

He also got up earlier in the morning, like today, just so he didn't fall behind. The mail would arrive soon. It had started coming first thing in the morning, and with it might be another letter for her—one that would send her away to a new town and a new potential husband.

He didn't want that. Not at all.

Rubbing his eyes tiredly, Peter opened his safe. There wasn't too much in there, but there was an item that needed to go into the mail delivery. The sound of a wagon caught his attention and he hurriedly grabbed the small sack that held the money the reverend had asked him to see got sent to the next town over.

The mail rider came in, dropped off the mail sack, and took the one Peter gave him. The entire transaction took less than a minute. The mail couldn't be delayed for anyone.

Peter turned his back to the door and yawned again. There was a lot of mail this morning. Two sacks full. He'd need to hurry to get it sorted before people started coming to see if they had letters.

The door opened again. Without turning around, Peter asked, "Forget something, Harry?"

Harry didn't answer. Peter started to turn, when something struck him from behind. Peter fell to the ground and reached around for something to defend himself.

A dark figure vaulted over the counter, knocking the mailbags over. He grabbed at the safe, but it was bolted to the ground. Through his pain, Peter lunged forward, grabbing the high stool he often sat on. He pushed it toward the robber, and there was a yelp of pain, then the stool was kicked back into Peter. The robber tried to leave, but Peter grabbed onto his leg.

The attacker swung at Peter, kicking him twice, then pushing him away. Peter threw himself once more at the attacker, but the man, bigger than he was, grabbed him and slammed Peter into the wall, before bolting out the door.

Peter's vision was blurry, and his head was pounding, but he managed to stumble out of the post office door and into the street. His legs were wobbly, and his hip couldn't seem to support his weight. He collapsed into the street, wishing he could call for help. Wishing his leg didn't ache so he could have run for help.

Peter felt as though he were far away. There were sounds, shouts, but he couldn't tell if he was imagining them. Everything sounded so faint. He tried to move himself, but his limbs were too heavy. His aching hip wouldn't work.

"Hold still, lad," Hank's voice said, close by.

Then, someone shouted loudly. He couldn't tell who.

"Get the doctor! Bring him to the café. Hurry!"

Peter felt himself being raised up, and through his blurry vision he could see people around him. Several men carried him to the café, and he heard a familiar voice gasp, "Peter!"

He wanted to tell Alyssa it was okay. That he was okay. But he wasn't sure it was true.

Something warm dripped down his cheek and he could sense it was blood. Peter teetered in and out of consciousness, and couldn't remember when they'd set him down, but he knew he was in a bed, and the reverend, Hank, and the doctor were close to him, talking in low voices.

"...saw him lying in the street," Hank said.

"The post office was robbed," Gabriel added.

"...blood loss. Possible concussion," the doctor said.

Peter tried to talk. To ask them to be quiet, to not alarm Alyssa. But his lips wouldn't move. His legs wouldn't move. His arms were too heavy.

A thick liquid was put into his mouth and the pain lessened. His vision was clearing, and the last thing Peter saw was Alyssa's beautiful face covered in tears as she leaned close to him.

Chapter 13

Alyssa stood, wringing her hands as she listened to the townsfolk. There was an impromptu meeting at the café, and everyone seemed to be talking at once.

"Quiet! Quiet down," Hank demanded, his voice booming and filling the room.

Everyone quieted immediately, and Gabriel and Laura moved closer to him. Alyssa listened as he began to speak.

"You all know we have no sheriff," Hank started, "but you also all know that I'm the acting sheriff, seeing as that's what I've done before. Now, yes, it's true. Someone attacked Peter West, our postmaster. Doc says he'll be fine, but he got beaten up pretty badly. The man who did it is on the run. Could be hiding here in the town even." Hank stopped, and made a point of squinting at each person.

"I'll be keeping a close eye out, and I expect anyone with any news to come to me right away, night or day."

The crowd murmured in agreement.

"When you find him, lock him up," a woman's shrill voice said.

"That's right!" an old man agreed. "Anyone who'd hurt Peter is a criminal indeed."

A third voice called out, "And if someone would do that to Peter, they might do that or worse to any one of us."

The room burst into chatter again, but Hank didn't stop them. Instead, he sighed to Gabriel, "This isn't looking good. I can't think any of these folks here would have done it, so we need to be vigilant and on the lookout for a stranger."

Gabriel winked at Laura. "Time for you to think of a plan, just in case," he told her.

Laura laughed. "I will," she promised. "But first, Doc, how is he, really?"

The doctor, a man who looked to be in his late thirties, shook his head. "Rest is what he needs. Hurt him pretty bad." Alyssa creeped closer to hear better. "A deep cut in his forehead, a good number of bruises. He'll be okay, but might be in bed for a few days. I'll check on him in the morning."

"Was anything stolen?" Alyssa asked. She was trying very hard to contain the fury that rose within her. "I don't understand why anyone would have attacked him."

The reverend sighed. "That might have been my fault. I thought I'd kept it quiet, but perhaps not. Peter was keeping a donation to the town next over in his safe. It was raised by the church to help after a fire. I saw the mail wagon leave, so I'm sure it made it away safely, but the thief must have known it was there, and not realized it was leaving on the mail wagon."

"Then we will keep an eye on the post office," Hank said. "Perhaps they will return to look for it."

"I suggest we leave everything as it is," Gabriel said. "Even though it's a mess, and simply watch. If someone returns, we will capture them. Let them think we are too worried about Peter to worry about the mail." He looked at Laura then. "What do you think?"

"I think it's a good plan," she agreed.

Maggie crossed her arms. "Makes me angry, someone disrupting our town like this. There's no good reason, none at all, to go and steal from honest folks and leave a man wounded. Thank goodness he managed to crawl into the street. Might have been a while before we'd known, otherwise."

Alyssa hugged her arms around herself. She was feeling sick with worry over Peter and furious at whoever had done this. The combination was too much, and she glanced around for a place to sit. Maggie looked over at her and wrapped an arm around her shoulders. "Don't you worry none. Our doc is good. Peter will be fine."

"Can I go sit with him?" Alyssa asked.

"That's a good idea," Maggie agreed. "I'm closing the café for the rest of the day."

Alyssa went up the stairs and to the room Peter had been moved to. He was so pale it alarmed her. There was a large bandage on his forehead, and it had already soaked through with crimson blood.

"He'll need that changed every few hours," the doctor said behind her. "Let me show you how."

Watching carefully, Alyssa took note of how to clean and rebandage the wound, then sat herself down in a chair in the corner. Laura joined her for a time, and when she left, Maggie came up with a tray containing a simple meal for the both of them.

"Should he be sleeping?" Alyssa asked, as she gratefully accepted the tea. "I know the doctor said it wasn't a concussion, but it still makes me wonder."

"I don't know," Maggie confessed. "I suppose the doc knows what he's doing. We have to trust in it, anyway."

Alyssa nodded. She hated feeling helpless. It was a terrible thing to want to help someone but not know how.

They sat there for several hours. Maggie worked on her knitting and Alyssa drew. She was trying to keep her mind off her worry, but it wasn't working.

Every now and then, they gave Peter water to drink, dribbling it through his lips, though he slept soundly. It was likely the medicine the doctor had given him, and Alyssa hoped in the morning he'd be much improved.

When it was finally dark, the reverend appeared. He explained that he and Hank were taking turns with a few other men watching the post office. Until it was his turn, he'd stay with Peter, so that the women could rest. Alyssa didn't really want to leave, but she climbed into bed, eyes wide open.

She kept wondering who had done this. Was it one of the teenagers who had called him names? A person just passing through? Could it have been one of the people in the town? She didn't know any of them very well, but that was a possibility, she supposed.

Dawn came, and though she'd have usually admired the canvas nature was painting with dusky purple and blues turning into crimsons and oranges, this morning she was more focused on Peter.

Hurriedly she dressed, and got to his room at the same time Maggie did with a breakfast tray. The two ate and talked quietly while Peter slept. The doctor arrived a short time later and examined him. Peter stirred and opened his eyes.

"Doc?" he croaked.

"Take it easy," the doctor said, checking the wound on Peter's head. "Just hold still. I'm examining your head. How do you feel?"

"Like someone bested me in a brawl," Peter groaned, his eyes closed.

"That's about what happened," the doctor said, chuckling and leaning back. He checked Peter's pulse and then looked at Alyssa. "Hand me that bottle there," he told her.

She moved closer, handed him the small green bottle he had indicated, then stood to the side as he cleaned then re-bandaged the head wound. Peter's eyes fluttered. He wasn't fully awake; it seemed it was an effort to even move slightly.

Tears filled Alyssa's eyes. Who could have done this? And why? She impatiently waited while the doctor finished with Peter. He quietly left the room with Maggie, and she moved her chair closer.

"Peter," Alyssa whispered. "If you can hear me, please, get better quickly. I-I don't know what I would do without you in my life. You have become so very dear to me, and it's making my heart hurt to see you like this."

Hot tears fell down her cheeks, and she reached for his hand. She squeezed it gently, but there was no response from him. "Peter," Alyssa whispered. "I think...I think I love you."

Chapter 14

Peter blinked a few times and waited for his tired eyes to clear enough so he could see. There had been the strangest of dreams in his mind, of shouts and a fight, and then an angel hovering over him. As he gained his focus, Peter was surprised to see he was in a room he didn't recognize.

Where was he?

The bed felt different. He was sure his pillows had never been so soft, nor the mattress so comfortable. He could stay here happily for a long time. But...where was here?

Before he could wonder more, the angel, the woman whose soft touch he'd felt often on his head or hand, came into view. He blinked in surprise. Alyssa?

"Oh! Peter," she gasped. "You are awake. How do you feel?"

How did he feel? Peter wasn't quite sure. Experimentally, he moved an arm and groaned as first stiffness, then pain shot up his shoulder.

"Don't move," Alyssa ordered, and she ran from the room. Peter could hear her on the stairs, and her faint voice calling, "He's awake!"

Shortly thereafter, there were more people crammed in the small room than Peter could have thought possible. Everyone was silent, their attention focused on him, and it made Peter feel just a little uncomfortable, and at the same time surprised. He knew his friends were always concerned for his wellbeing, but this seemed very different.

Alyssa was near him, Maggie and Laura next to her. The doctor was inspecting him, while Hank and Gabriel stood close by. The shuffling of feet alerted him to the fact others must be outside the door as well.

Peter endured the pokes and inspection. After a half dozen grunts from the doctor, he finally asked, "Can anyone tell me where I am?"

"At the café," Hank told him. "I brought you here after I found you."

"Found me," Peter said. He was quiet for a moment, and felt the heavy weight of the collective gaze upon him. "I don't remember much," he said.

"I'll need to take a statement, if you are able," Hank said.

"A statement?" Peter repeated. "Am I...did I do something wrong?"

"Not you," Alyssa said, and reached for his hand. She sat next to him. "Someone tried to rob the post office. You fought him off, got very injured, and he got away."

Peter sucked in a sharp breath. "So that's what happened. I wondered why he was attacking me."

Gabriel cleared his throat. "I'm worried it was because they knew about the money for the town over."

"Don't worry," Peter assured him. "I saw that safely myself to the mail wagon. It will get there, if it's not already."

Gabriel nodded, then shook his head. "I still feel guilt. I'll deliver anything like that myself, from now on."

"Nothing to feel badly for," Peter said. "It could have been any reason they wanted something in the post office."

"Yes, and it's a mess," Hank told him. He stepped forward with a small notebook and a pencil. "Can you tell me all you remember?"

The room was silent as Peter struggled to recall everything, and told the story in bits and pieces. When he was done, there were low voices. He tried to listen all at once, but it was making his head ache.

"I need to go see what's happened inside," Peter said. "It's my responsibility, and my job."

"If you spend the remainder of the day resting, then you can go tomorrow," the doctor told him.

"I'll go along with you," Hank said. "I'm acting sheriff again. Maybe it's time our town sends away for a real one."

"A problem for another day," Gabriel said. "I'll join you both tomorrow."

Alyssa said, "I will as well, so he doesn't overdo things." She looked at Peter then, and promised, "We'll help you get things right, and then get to the bottom of this."

The doctor ushered everyone out of the room, including, to his dismay, Alyssa. Peter laid in the bed staring up at the ceiling. He hoped Alyssa was right, and that they could get to the bottom of this. It wasn't exactly that he was afraid. No, from what his friends had explained, he'd held his own against the attacker and the man had fled. It was more he felt unsettled.

Things like this didn't happen in a small town like Deepwater. Chills came over him as he wondered just who had been in the post office, and why they'd attacked him. Was it really for the money in the safe? He wasn't sure, but Peter hoped the person would be caught soon. What if something happened to Alyssa? He had to get himself recovered, to look after her.

His door cracked open and his eyes widened to see Alyssa slipping inside. She had a small tray and left the door open behind her.

"I've gotten permission to see that you eat and assist if needed," she said softly, not quite meeting his eyes as she set the tray on a table near him.

When she turned, their eyes met, and Peter knew he was blushing from the heat that ran over his face. "Thank you," he said. Then, before he could help himself, he added, "Alyssa, I don't know if you should come tomorrow. I'm worried something may happen to you if the thief comes back. I couldn't stand it or ever forgive myself if you were hurt."

She settled next to him and offered him a mug of broth to start. With a thoughtful tone, she replied, "I think that's very sweet of you. I'm not concerned though. Hank and the reverend will be there, and you."

A smile formed then, and she said, leaning forward ever so slightly, "Truth be told, I almost wish he'd be there tomorrow. Whoever it was. While I don't think that would be the case, by the time I'd be done with them, there might not be much left for Hank to lock up."

Peter couldn't help it. He laughed. He knew every word she'd said was true, and he could just imagine her chasing after the robber. Alyssa joined in his laughter, and once she'd composed herself, said, "Laughter is the best medicine, my grandma used to say."

"Mine too," Peter grinned. "And I can see you chasing after whoever it is." His smile faded. "Just promise me you won't. That you'll be careful. They might be a dangerous criminal. I don't want you hurt."

"And I don't want you hurt," Alyssa said. She brushed her fingertips against his cheek, and leaned forward like she was about to kiss him.

Peter was hoping she might, when he heard footsteps on the stairs. Alyssa stood, smiled at him, and said, "I'll check on you later."

The phantom of her presence lingered once the door closed behind her. Peter ate slowly, then settled back in bed. He drifted off to sleep, having a dream where he and Alyssa were next to the stream, soaking up the sunshine and laughing and talking, and he read to her.

Peter glanced down and saw a ring on her finger. Did that mean she was married? His pleasant dream turned into a nightmare, as the stagecoach appeared, and a man cloaked in darkness grabbed Alyssa and hauled her away.

He woke in a sweat, his heart pounding. The words Gabriel had spoken to him just days before suddenly slammed into his mind.

"My friend," Gabriel had said, leaning closer with sympathy in his voice, "you must say something sooner rather than later. The day will arrive that the answer to her letter comes. It might even be something that takes her away shortly thereafter. Don't waste this chance that you have, this moment that may never repeat itself because you are scared."

Peter knew then, without a doubt. He was at a fork in the road. He could either confess his feelings to Alyssa and see if she felt the same, or he could stand by, heartbroken and helpless as she went away to a new life. That must have been what his dream was reminding him of.

But was there still time? Or was he too late?

Chapter 15

Alyssa watched as Peter tried not to rush out of the door. He had the approval of the doctor to go to the post office and see what condition it was in, and if anything had been stolen or damaged. It was obvious he was more than eager.

She had taken it upon herself to make sure that he wasn't overdoing himself. Though he had promised he felt better, Peter looked a little pale. His head was still bandaged, and as upset as all of that made Alyssa, the thing that concerned her the most was his worried look. In her short time there in Deepwater, she'd never seen Peter appear anything less than cheerful and relaxed. Right now, he was tense and anxious.

The post office was only a few more yards away, and Alyssa noticed that Hank was ushering people away from the front of it. Word must have gotten around Peter was coming to examine the damage. In small towns, anything out of the ordinary was exciting, and Alyssa suspected the crowd was also a little anxious. She knew she was.

Gabriel arrived then and fell into step with them. His appearance made Alyssa feel better. Peter seemed to relax slightly as well. Was that because Peter was friends with him? Or because Gabriel was a man of God? She wasn't sure. Perhaps it was a mixture of both, but either way, she was grateful he was there.

Hank stood waiting in front of the post office and offered Peter the key. "Took it from inside and locked up as soon as we got you settled," he said. "No one has been inside since."

"Thank you," Peter said. He shook his head, then winced. "I'm a little worried about what might greet me when I walk inside."

Alyssa reached for his hand. "Whatever it is, you aren't alone," she assured him. "We are here to help you set things to rights."

"Look at the outside first," Hank said, his notebook pulled out. "Tell me if you see anything out of the ordinary or anything damaged. I'm making note of it all. We'll build up a case for when your attacker is found."

With a small nod, Peter stood in front of the post office and carefully observed the front of the building. Alyssa took the time to do the same. She'd never really looked at the front of the small building. She was always in a hurry to get inside and see Peter.

Only about six paces wide and perhaps ten deep, the building was painted white, like most of those in the town, with a blue door. There was a mail window, a large opening with wooden shutters where someone could simply walk up to the outside of the building and ask for their mail or send it. They didn't need to go inside. Peter had explained most people used that unless the weather was poor, they wanted to talk for a while, or the mail delivery was there but unsorted.

"It all looks fine," Peter said, then placed the key into the lock.

When he pushed open the door, he groaned, and Alyssa saw why. It looked like a hurricane had gone through the building. Letters covered just about every surface—the floor, the counter, a chair that was overturned. The small safe was open, the door hanging wide, and it was empty.

"Should anything be in the safe?" Hank asked.

"No, it usually stays empty," Peter explained.

Gabriel stood quietly, like the rest of them, as they surveyed the room. "Do you see any damage? Other than the knocked over chair and stool?"

"I don't," Peter answered. "Surprisingly. It's going to take a little effort to get these letters picked up though."

"Let me," Alyssa said. She began to gather the envelopes and put them into a neat stack. Fortunately, none of them appeared to be torn. Several had small crumples or a footprint, but nothing that would prevent the recipient from reading the letter.

Gabriel was righting the chair and stool, while Hank asked Peter to show where the attack had taken place, and what he had done.

"I feel as though the whole thing is my fault," Gabriel murmured, standing close to her.

Alyssa looked at him in surprise. She didn't think a reverend would ever feel bad or guilty or anything else about, well, anything. "It wasn't your fault," she told him.

"Perhaps I didn't do the act," he answered. "But I feel responsibility. I put Peter into the position of sending out those funds, and I cannot help but wonder, was it someone in the town? Did I let them down? Not listen when they needed a friend to talk to? Did I not notice someone was in such a dire situation that I could have prevented it?"

"You can't blame yourself," Alyssa told him. "I hardly know you, but I do know you are a good man."

"I appreciate that," Gabriel told her with a smile. "I could say the same. I don't know you well, but I am glad you are here in Deepwater. You are just what this town—and Peter—need."

Alyssa picked up another letter and looked at it before putting it into the pile. "That is kind of you. I enjoy the town and its people. But as for Peter..." she glanced at

Peter, who was pointing to the door, "it's complicated. I was sent here to marry someone else by a mail-order agency."

"But you didn't," Gabriel said.

"No, however, I wrote to the agency to explain what happened, and they are supposed to find me someone else. I might not have a say over what I do. I signed a contract. My word means a great deal to me. If I am promised, then I must go. Besides, Peter and I are friends, nothing more." She picked up another letter and then froze. This one had very familiar letters on it. She looked closely again and frowned. "This is for me," she said softly.

Though her voice was barely above a whisper, Peter seemed to sense her distress and walked over. He glanced at the letter in her hand. "Yes. It's for you," he told her quietly. "It's from the mail-order agency." He pointed to the name on the back of the envelope.

Gabriel silently squeezed her arm and stepped away to give them privacy. Taking a deep breath, Alyssa tried to still her suddenly trembling fingers. "I'll save this for later," she said, and pushed it into her pocket.

The letter had arrived too soon. She wasn't ready. Not to leave, not to find a husband. Alyssa took another deep breath. What would the letter say? Would it tell her to continue to wait, or had a potential husband been found? Her heart was racing and her stomach felt uneasy.

She couldn't tell what Peter was thinking, but wished she knew. When she'd told the reverend that she and Peter were only friends, what she hadn't said was she wished it could be more.

Peter had a distant look in his eyes and a sad look on his face. She rested her hand on his arm. "Is this too much for you? Being here? Perhaps we should go back so you can rest."

"No, I'm fine," Peter sighed. "I mean, it's just a lot. Being here, seeing this. Seeing that letter."

Alyssa stilled. The room seemed to close in on her. Her throat grew tight. "Peter," she said, at the same time he said her name.

They each paused, laughed, and then Peter opened his mouth to speak when Hank walked back inside and they were no longer alone. "Whelp," he said. "Nothing's missing, you say. The back of the building looks good. I suspect that someone was looking for money. Deepwater is a small town, and only newly turned into a stage stop, so it's not likely the person knew there was no payroll kept there like many post offices do. Could very well have been someone who left on the stage, as there was one that day."

"Could be," Peter agreed.

They both moved toward the door, and Alyssa started to follow when she spotted a pair of Peter's shoes next to a jacket. A flutter of excitement filled her. This was her chance! If she could just sneak one of his shoes, the one for the foot that had been injured and made him limp, then she'd be able to take it to the shoemaker.

Peter and Gabriel walked outside, where a small cluster of town folks had gathered, and were looking anxiously at Hank. Alyssa bit her lip. She didn't want Peter to be upset about a missing shoe. But, if she didn't take it now, she'd likely not have another chance, especially if she had to leave.

She pretended to drop her letter, and then, with a quick look at the door, picked up both the letter and the shoe. She wished there was something to hide it in, but there wasn't, so she simply held her arm along her side and pressed the shoe into her skirt, wrapping the material around it. It looked strange, but she'd hurry to the café soon. Perhaps no one would notice her holding her arm so awkwardly.

Even if they did, she was hoping no one would be so rude as to ask.

"Anything we need to know?" the blacksmith was asking as she walked outside.

"Only that we will continue to keep an eye out, but at this time I don't feel like there's a threat," Hank assured the crowd.

"Remain vigilant, but do not be fearful," Gabriel added. "There's no need to eye your neighbor and suspect anyone."

"Easier said than done," an old woman said. "If they'd attack Peter, they'd attack anyone."

"They weren't attacking me, specifically," Peter said, trying to reassure the crowd. "I had money in the safe that day for transport, and word must have gotten around."

There were nods and mummers. That they understood. Not a week went by without word of a stagecoach robbery or some other theft, even in smaller towns. That's just how it was.

The men stood there talking to the crowd, and Alyssa knew this was her chance to escape and get the shoe to the shoemaker.

"Peter," Alyssa whispered, leaning in closely, "I must return to the café. I'll check on you soon. I know you want to work today to sort the letters and put things back to a semblance of normal, but please, don't overwork yourself."

Before he could answer, she had vanished. As Alyssa hurried away, she felt a little guilty. It was for a good reason that she'd stolen his shoe, she told herself. Now, all she had to do was get the shoe safely to the shoemaker and see if her idea would work.

Chapter 16

As Alyssa hurried away, Peter sighed. He wondered what was in the letter Alyssa received. He wanted to offer to read it to her, both to ease her mind and his, but there had been a lot of people around and he was nervous. Also, he wasn't sure if Alyssa wanted anyone knowing that she didn't know how to read.

So, as he returned to the post office to sort the stack of letters once more, he decided there wasn't anything at all he could do. Except just worry over it.

That's what he did for the next hour. When the doctor stopped by and urged him back to the café and bed, Peter nodded, and then picked up his jacket that had been hanging on a peg. It was a little cool outside. As he turned to leave, he stopped and turned back, frowning. One of his spare shoes he kept there was missing.

Peter looked under the stool and the chair. He leaned down to check under the counter. Curious, he wandered the entire post office, looking for the shoe. It had been there earlier today, and shoes couldn't just walk away—not without feet—so Peter was more than a little confused. Too tired to worry about it more, he stopped looking. His head was starting to ache and he didn't want to make it worse.

He locked the post office behind him and placed the key into his pocket. Unfortunately, this wasn't the first time something of his had gone missing. Chances were, one of those teenagers was playing a prank on him. The shoe would turn up later or it wouldn't. Not much he could do about it. Thankfully, it was an old pair and he didn't wear them often. Still, it was rather strange. Why only take one shoe? What good would that do someone?

On his way to the café, Peter felt reassured when he saw Hank organizing an evening patrol. The men of Deepwater hadn't stopped keeping a watchful eye. Luckily, there had not been any issues, but he was going to be wary himself for a while. He wished there was more he could do to help. No one would let him though, saying he was still recovering.

In truth, he was. He didn't let on that he ached as much as he did, but Peter gratefully opened the café door and returned to the room Maggie had placed him in. He fell asleep, and woke a while later to a knock on the door. When he opened it, he was struck by a delightful smell. It tickled his senses and made his mouth water.

"Brought you some lunch," Gabriel said cheerfully. "Laura made it especially for you."

"That was kind of her," Peter said. "Won't you come in?"

Gabriel set down a basket and uncovered it. "Fried chicken, fresh biscuits, and a wedge of pie. Cherry, looks like."

Peter's stomach rumbled loudly.

"Tuck in," Gabriel said. "I wanted to visit a little. See how you were after your trip to the post office today."

Peter ate a bite of the chicken, and thought. How *was* he? After a moment of consideration, he decided to tell the truth. "It's not been a great day. There's a lot on my mind. I'm worried the person will come back. I'm also upset. Why the post office? Why me? The money you had to go the next town over wasn't so much that even a criminal would have killed for it. Was there another reason they were there, or was it coincidence? I'm not sure I'll feel at ease until I have answers."

Gabriel rubbed at his chin and nodded. "I agree. All you said is true. It wasn't a large amount. Which is why I'm concerned it's not a stranger. We are all keeping watch. If the person is going to try and steal again, I have the feeling it will be soon."

"What makes you so sure?" Peter asked.

"I was a highwayman myself, remember?" Gabriel laughed. "I still think like one. That's how I help protect people."

"That's right," Peter said. "I'd almost forgotten." He continued eating the chicken. "Please tell Laura this is the best I've ever had."

"I will," Gabriel promised. Then he gave Peter a look that made him feel like squirming.

"What?" Peter asked.

"Feeling anything else?" Gabriel asked.

"Not really," Peter shrugged. He really didn't want to talk about anything more. It was bad enough admitting that he was rattled by the attack.

"Oh? Not even about Aylssa getting that letter?" his friend raised an eyebrow.

Peter sat down the biscuit he'd just picked up. Sighing heavily, he looked at it. He knew Gabriel. The man wouldn't stop until he answered. "Maybe."

"My friend, she likes you," Gabriel said. "Need I remind you that hesitating to speak up can cause the loss of a friendship, and something that could grow into more?"

"It's not that simple," Peter said.

"Because you aren't letting it be," Gabriel said.

A flash of anger went through Peter. "How could it be? She came here to marry someone. When that didn't work, she sent away a letter to find someone else. That someone else isn't me. I've no right to interfere in her plans."

"You don't know what her plans are, though," Gabriel said.

The truth tumbled out of Peter's lips before he could stop them. "They sure aren't with a man like me. I'm not the kind of person she'd want. She needs someone brave and strong, someone to take care of her. Someone who can provide better for her than I can."

"I wouldn't be so sure," Gabriel said. "You are plenty brave. You fought back when you were attacked."

"Self preservation," Peter muttered. "That's all."

"I don't believe that," Gabriel said. "Besides, there's a difference between being scared and doing what you have to do, and being scared and running. You didn't run."

"No, no, I didn't," Peter said thoughtfully. "I'm not sure that makes me brave, but I'll think about what you said."

Gabriel stood and clapped Peter's shoulder. "Don't let what I said upset you. I meant for it to encourage you."

"I know," Peter muttered. "Doesn't mean that I like hearing it, though."

"Laura says I talk too much," Gabriel sighed. "It's true. Sometimes I don't know when to stop."

"Now would be good," Peter said, then he grinned, so his friend would understand he was joking.

Gabriel laughed. "I've got to head on. A sermon to practice."

"What's the topic?" Peter asked.

"You'll have to wait until Sunday," Gabriel winked. "Wouldn't want you thinking I was lecturing you." He moved to the door, and then, his voice serious, said, "You have all you need inside you. We all do. You just have to find it."

Peter held back a groan at the parting words of wisdom Gabriel always seemed to impart, and then called after him, "Don't forget to thank Laura for me."

Gabriel waved his hand in acknowledgment as he went down the stairs, and Peter returned to his room. As each bite of cherry pie burst in his mouth, he couldn't help but wonder. Would Alyssa stay? What might he need to do to convince her? Even if she was only there as his friend, at least she'd be here.

He decided the idea was worth continued thought. Standing, Peter caught sight of Laura's basket. Gabriel had accidently left it. "I'd better return this," he said. "A walk will clear my mind."

The café was empty when he got downstairs, and he was a little disappointed that he didn't see Alyssa. Hadn't she said she was coming back here? Peter felt a surge of worry. Maybe she was avoiding him. He wouldn't be surprised.

His shoulders slumped, Peter set out for the church. He'd never felt so confused in his life. He wanted to be fearless. To tell Alyssa how he felt. But that wasn't him. He wasn't like a hero in a book. Someone bold and daring.

In the distance, the sound of children playing caught his attention, and he smiled as two young boys dueled with swords made of branches. He remembered playing pretend when he was that age. He'd always felt so strong and special. The other children had looked to him as the leader to make up games, and he'd always done something where they were heroes.

Peter paused. What was it Gabriel had said? That he had all he needed inside of him already? He just had to find it?

He walked up to the church steps, then a movement caught his eye. Over to the left of the building, a person was lurking in the shadows and prying the window open, right to the reverend's office.

Chapter 17

Alyssa sat at her favorite table in the café. The letter was before her and she was staring at it. She was scared to open it. Even more afraid to ask someone to read it to her. What would it say? Would there be a man waiting for her?

She traced the letters of her name with her finger and sighed. She hated this. The worry. It was better to just read the letter and face her situation head on. But she couldn't. Other than making out her name, she doubted she'd understand a single word in the envelope.

Standing, Alyssa walked over to the counter where Maggie was wiping down the top. She stopped, the letter in her hand suddenly seeming to weigh as much as a heavy sack of flour.

"Maggie," Alyssa asked shyly. "Would you please read this to me?"

The older woman looked at the envelope, and a flash of sympathy went through her eyes. "Of course, dear," she said. "Do you want us to go somewhere more private?"

Alyssa shook her head. "No, it's okay. I cannot imagine anything in there that's so personal others can't hear. Besides, we are alone right now."

Maggie nodded and opened the envelope. Paper money fell out, and Maggie moved it to the side. As she unfolded the letter, she set it down onto the counter and touched each of the words as she read it to Alyssa, just as Peter had before.

Dear Miss Moore,

We regret the unfortunate circumstances that you find yourself in. Please accept this money to pay for the expenses that you've incurred. Thank you for your patience as we took the time to find you another possible match.

As the contract you signed states, if for any reason that you decide not to marry, the only obligation on your end is to return the travel funds your intended groom sent. As Mr. Gerald Weatherbee was the one to break the contract, you do not need to refund any money.

There is another man who appears to be a suitable match. He is a tailor looking for a wife to help in his shop with sewing. He lives a simple life and is not very well off, but he says he can provide for all of your needs.

If you should choose to accept his offer, please return a letter to us, and we will forward you the tickets to arrive to him, and a small sum of money for your travel expenses.

However, if you no longer wish to be placed into marriage by our company, please write back and let us know that as well. Regardless, this sum is yours to cover your expenses while you waited to hear from us.

We wish you the best in whatever you choose.

Kind regards,

The Marston Mail-Order Bride Agency.

Maggie finished reading and glanced at Alyssa. "Would you like me to read it again?" she asked.

"No," Alyssa said. She sat down on a stool in front of the counter and rested her cheek on a hand.

"At least they've sent you money for your expenses," Maggie said, with a forced note of cheerfulness.

"Yes. Please take what you are owed," Alyssa said. "And for the rest of the week."

Maggie nodded, and slipped part of the money into her apron pocket. She pushed the rest toward Alyssa. "This is yours," she said.

Alyssa didn't look at it as she nodded. Her stomach hurt. Here it was. The time to decide. They'd found a husband for her. She could go to him if she wished. A tailor. She could spend her days sewing. Her needs provided for. But something didn't feel right about it.

"I don't know what to do," Alyssa said softly. "I don't feel right about going. But I don't know if staying here, seeking work and trying to build a life is the right decision, either."

"You don't need to choose today," Maggie assured her. "It's a lot to think about, and you need to take your time doing so."

"Yes," Alyssa sighed. She wanted to say more. To talk more, but she felt numb inside. It was difficult to speak, let alone form coherent thoughts. Her mind was in shock. While she knew the letter would come eventually, when it actually arrived, she was not prepared.

Alyssa stood, and her stool scraped as it slid back. "I think I will go for a walk," she said, and scooped up the money and the envelope. Maggie handed her the letter and Alyssa hurried to her room for her wrap. She wasn't sure if there was a chill in the air, or if she was simply shaken up and that's why she was suddenly shivering.

It wasn't but a moment later she left the café, Peter's shoe wrapped in a bit of brown paper she'd had. Alyssa made her way to where she'd seen the shoemaker's shop. She hoped he'd be there. And hoped he wouldn't ask many questions. Such as, why did she have Peter's shoe, and did he know.

Most of all, she hoped he would listen, truly listen, and help with this possibly ridiculous idea.

Alyssa paused before his shop a moment later, and then resolutely pushed open the door. She still felt guilt over having Peter's shoe. But the sooner she got this done, the sooner she could return it. Perhaps, even without him knowing about it.

Taking one more deep breath, Alyssa walked inside. The shoemaker looked up and greeted her. "Hello, how can I help you?" he asked.

Alyssa set the brown paper bundle on the shop counter. "I don't know if you can. But I'm hoping so. You see...I have an idea. Do you know Mr. West, the postmaster?"

"Sure do," the shoemaker said. "Everyone knows Peter."

"Right." Alyssa let out a breath. "Well, I made an observation of how he limps. And then I had an idea of how to help him with that."

"I'm not a doctor," the shoemaker said, looking puzzled.

"He doesn't need a doctor," Alyssa said, and pulled the shoe from the paper. "I think what he needs is a shoe repair. Or an addition to it."

"Go on," the shoemaker said, as he picked up Peter's shoe and examined it.

"You see, I was having tea with Laura—the reverend's wife?" At his nod, she continued. "Her kitchen table was wobbling. She leaned over and put a small piece of wood under it, and it stopped. It evened up the table legs."

"Ah! I think I see now," the shoemaker said. He rubbed at an ear. "It will be tricky not knowing how much I need to add to the heel, but I think..." He picked up the shoe and began holding strips of leather against it.

Alyssa watched for a moment before asking, "But you think something can be done?"

"I do," agreed the shoemaker. "Leave this with me. I'll start tonight."

"Thank you," Alyssa said. "Please, though. It's a secret. Don't tell him."

"Wouldn't dream of it," the man smiled. "Come back to see me tomorrow."

Alyssa opened her purse then. "I'm happy to pay in advance if you need me to."

"No," the shoemaker said. "No charge. First, I need to see if I can even do this. Next, I make Peter's shoes already. This should be included. Lastly, it's Peter. I wouldn't dream of charging him. He does a lot of good around this place. He's always giving of himself and his time. I'm pleased I can do something for him."

Alyssa smiled. "Thank you," she said.

The shoemaker was already at his bench taking measurements, so she left.

She continued through the door and back out onto the street, when she heard the church bell clanging in alarm. Men were racing toward the building while women in their long skirts hurried behind.

Worriedly, Alyssa followed them. What had happened?

Chapter 18

Peter didn't hesitate when he saw the figure prying open the window to the church. It was obvious to him that the person was up to no good, or else they'd have gone through the doors and into the chapel that way.

"Hey!" he yelled.

The person turned, their hat low and covering most of their face. He bolted away, around the side of the church and toward the woods.

Where Laura and Gabriel lived.

Peter took off after him, dropping the basket he'd held. He knew Laura would be home, but he wasn't sure about Gabriel. He couldn't let danger come to her.

His leg slowed him, as it always did. There was a burning sensation in his hip as it fought him. His legs pumped as hard as they could, trying to keep up with the man who was running, circling back now around the church. An idea came to Peter then, and he stopped running and switched directions.

Just as he'd hoped, the man ran right toward him, and Peter was able to close the gap. He threw himself at the figure and yelled, "Thief! Help!"

The man pushed at him, then hit him, but Peter held on with all of his strength. His head was aching, and he had a sinking feeling he'd split the wound open again. He wrestled with the thief, and was relieved to hear the sound of racing footfalls headed in his direction.

"Grab him," Hank yelled, and a crush of people descended upon them. Peter was helped up, and the would-be robber surrounded.

"What happened?" Hank demanded.

"I was returning something to the Sullivans," Peter said, noticing the basket on the ground and picking it up. "He was prying open a window to the reverend's office."

"Explain yourself," Hank said sternly.

The prisoner refused to talk. He looked down, his jaw clenched.

"Put him in the holding cell," Hank said.

"No! Please!" the prisoner said. He looked up then, and Peter caught sight of a young man, not much older than a boy. Tears had filled his eyes. "Please don't," he begged.

Gabriel hurried forward then. "What's all this?" he asked.

"Peter caught him trying to break into your office," Hank said. "Taking him to be held. We'll get a judge to figure this out." He glared at the young man. "Were you the one who broke into the post office too?"

"Well, yes, but I didn't mean—"

Hank had heard enough and motioned for them to take the boy to the holding cell. Half the town was there, it seemed, watching as he was dragged through the street and locked up.

Peter stopped Gabriel. "I want to talk to him. He doesn't seem the sort to have meant malice. I think something else is going on."

"I agree," Gabriel said. "And we will, but Hank will be there too, as witness." Then he winced. "And perhaps you should get cleaned up first. Your head is bleeding and your shirt is torn."

Peter looked down. Sure enough, his shirt was torn at the sleeve. He held a hand to his head. "Bad enough I should go now?" he asked.

"Bad enough you don't want Maggie or Miss Moore to see you," Gabriel grinned.

He winced. "Good point." He handed over the basket and turned to hurry and get cleaned up when he heard a gasp.

It was too late. Maggie and Alyssa were rushing over.

"Peter," Alyssa said, her soft hands on his face in an instant. "You're bleeding."

"He stopped a robbery," Gabriel said. "So don't scold him."

"Are you hurt?" Alyssa asked, as her eyes searched him. "Your shirt is torn."

"It is," he agreed. "But I can mend it. I think."

"Nonsense. I will. What happened?" she asked.

Peter blinked. Alyssa had tucked her arm through his. Had she noticed she'd done it? He was feeling a bit numb. Thankfully, Gabriel took over.

"It appears we might have caught the man who attacked Peter and tried to steal from the post office," Gabriel explained. "We were about to go talk to him. But, Maggie, would you bring him something to eat and drink?"

Maggie looked like she was about to argue, but something in the reverend's expression must have made her reconsider. "Alyssa," she said, "you come along with me and help." Alyssa nodded and released Peter. A wave of disappointment washed over him. "We'll bring it right there," she said to Gabriel.

Was he mistaken that she also seemed disappointed to leave? Peter hoped not. He followed Gabriel into the small building that the town had received funds for to make a small jail, since the stage sometimes had prisoners aboard it. It had come in handy a few times to house their own criminals while waiting for the law to assist.

Pater studied the young man behind the bars. He couldn't have been eighteen. Though he was tall and lanky, he had a look of youth about him, no matter he tried growing a thin beard to make himself look older.

"I don't know you," Gabriel said by way of greeting. "I'm Reverend Gabriel Sulivan." He waited for the other to speak. Hank stood nearby, watching and listening.

"Jason Dawson," the prisoner said. "I'm sorry. I wasn't trying to hurt anyone. I was just hungry. I thought—" He lowered his head, his voice low, "Doesn't matter what I thought. Wrong is wrong. Stealing's a crime. I know that. I knew that. I shouldn't have done it."

"Why didn't you ask someone for help?" Gabriel asked, his posture easy as he pulled up a chair and sat opposite of Jason, who was sitting on the ground.

"I'm a stranger," Jason answered, looking at him in surprise.

"Not anymore," Gabriel said. "We've introduced ourselves. That makes us friends."

Jason looked confused, and then glanced at Peter, who shrugged, and Hank, who said, "Don't even try to figure it out. That's how he is. Goes with the job, I reckon."

Gabriel laughed. "Maybe so," he agreed. "But the fact remains, anyone in this town would have helped you or shown you where to go to get help. You've gotten yourself into a mess of trouble, young man."

"I know," Jason said, his voice quiet. "I made a lot of mistakes. It's harder than I thought, being out on my own."

"Why are you?" Gabriel asked.

"Don't have any folks," Jason said. "Been on my own for a while."

"I understand how that is," Gabriel said. "That happened to me too."

"I'm sorry," Jason said, looking at Peter. "I didn't mean to hurt you. Please, can you forgive me?"

Peter nodded. "I will," he said. "No harm done."

That wasn't exactly the truth, but he wouldn't hold a grudge. Right now, he wasn't sure what to think. The thief had turned out to be someone very different than he'd thought. From what any of them expected, really.

Just then, Maggie and Alyssa returned, bringing food. Hank gave it to Jason who ate hungrily. Maggie stood watching, hands on her hips while Alyssa stood next to Peter.

"What's going on?" she whispered.

Peter took Alyssa's hand and led her away. Once they were outside, he turned and gave her a grin. "I have the feeling Gabriel's going to talk for a while. Would you like to go for a walk?"

"I'd like that," Alyssa said with a smile. She squeezed his hand gently, and Peter blushed, happy she hadn't let go.

They walked slowly through the town, then by the stream. Neither had said anything. What Peter wanted to ask, was about the letter. The question burned in him. Filled him with worry. But how could he ask?

Alyssa paused at the spot they'd met the first time. She turned to him. It was as if she knew what he wanted to ask. "I opened the letter," she said. "Maggie read it to me."

"Oh?" Peter hoped he sounded nonchalant. Like he wasn't concerned.

"Yes. The agency found me an offer." Alyssa didn't say more, and Peter wondered what was going through her mind. She was looking away, and her face showed her mind was distant.

"W-what will you do?" Peter asked. He closed his eyes for a moment. What would she do? That was a foolish question. She'd take it, of course. Alyssa was a beautiful woman, one who was clever and talented. She needed someone like that. Not a person like him, someone with a limp and a stutter. While she might still be holding his hand, it was in friendship, nothing more. Of that, he was sure.

She sighed, deep and long. "I don't know." Sadness washed over her face. "I'm thinking still. He's...he's a tailor. I'd sew for him."

Peter gently squeezed her hand again. "Let's go back to the café," he said. "It's been a long day."

"Yes, of course," Alyssa said. "You need to change your shirt and rebandage your head. Then, can you stay for some cider? Do you feel up for that? We could...just talk."

"I'd like that," Peter said. Then he grinned at her, "That way, we also learn what will happen with the prisoner, and when the doctor stops by, he can see I'm not overdoing it."

"That is a good idea," she agreed.

They were soon at the café, and Maggie set mugs of cider and applesauce cake in front of them once Peter had returned from his temporary room.

Alyssa leaned close. "Could we have another lesson tomorrow? If you are feeling able? I have something I want to give you. In private."

Peter forced a smile on his face. "Of course," he told her. "Anything for you."

Oh, how he meant that. He'd walk the ends of the earth for Alyssa. He'd do anything for her. Anything to make her stay.

Then why don't you tell her that?

The voice whispered through his mind, and Peter started to dismiss it when the door to the café opened. Instinctively, he and Alyssa turned their heads to it, and he saw her stiffen, then a look of pure anger wash over her face as a large man, one he didn't know, strode toward her.

"There you are," he said. "Been looking for you."

Alyssa stood. "Mr. Weatherbee," she said cooly. "Our business is complete."

Business? What was she talking about? Peter glanced between the two of them, and saw Maggie, a look of fury on her own face, drawing closer.

"I've decided," the man continued, as if she hadn't spoken, "that I acted in haste. I'll take you. Have the reverend marry us today."

"You'll do nothing of the sort," Alyssa said, her voice filled with anger. She pointed a finger at him. "This potential marriage might have started with you rejecting me, but now *I* am rejecting *you*."

Peter was sure he was gaping. This was the man she was supposed to have married? He was about to say something when Maggie pointed her own finger and raised her voice.

"Out! Don't you come in my café again," she snapped at him. "You aren't welcome now nor ever. Miss Moore isn't interested in you one bit. The agency has already given her another man—a far better one if you ask me—and she'll have nothing more to do with you."

Just then, Hank walked in. "Trouble?" he asked, resting a hand at his hip on the gunbelt he now wore.

Peter stepped closer to the man, putting himself between him and Alyssa. "I don't think so. Yet," he said, his voice calm, but his gaze hard. "But it's good you are here, Hank. It appears there was a misunderstanding of sorts. Aly—Miss Moore isn't yours. You can leave, or you can be removed. The choice is yours. But you'd better make it fast."

Alyssa's former suitor glanced between each of them. He started to speak, when Peter took another step forward. His heart was pounding, but he would let himself get hurt before he ever let Alyssa go with a man like that.

Mr. Weatherbee must have sensed it, for he turned and left, wordlessly. The moment he was gone, Alyssa collapsed into her chair.

"There, there," Maggie soothed, rushing over to her. "We won't let him near you, love."

"Thank you," Alyssa said. Her words were for everyone, but her eyes...they were focused on him. Peter felt his stomach fluttering.

And then, when the voice whispered once again that he should tell her how he felt, he agreed. Maggie's words rang in his mind. She had another offer. A far better one.

It was time to show Alyssa that something even better was right here. That she didn't need to leave.

Chapter 19

Alyssa faced Maggie, squeezing the small package that held what she hoped would be the device to ease Peter's pain. "What if he gets upset that I've meddled in his business?" she worried.

"He won't," Maggie assured her.

"I hope not," she sighed. "I don't understand him. After Mr. Wetherbee was here, I thought—well, never mind what I thought."

Maggie gave her a sympathetic look. "He does like you," she told her. "He's just not good at saying so."

Alyssa nodded. Maggie was likely right. But that didn't make a difference. If Peter didn't admit that he liked her, then her decision must be made to accept the other offer of marriage, and gamble her future upon that. Why, oh why, wouldn't he say something? Tears of frustration filled her eyes.

"He'll be waiting," Maggie said.

Alyssa nodded. She started to the door, when Maggie called, "You know, you could just be the one to tell him how you feel."

Her cheeks heated. Alyssa didn't answer, but the entire short walk to the stream she wondered. Should she? Ought she?

Peter was waiting, and jumped up when he saw her. "Hello," he said, coming over.

"Hello," Alyssa answered, feeling shy all of a sudden. She fidgeted with the bundle.

"What's that?" Peter asked.

"It's for you," she blurted out, and thrust it toward him. As he reached for it, she pulled it back. "But you must promise me you won't be upset with me."

"Upset with you?" Peter looked at her, confused.

"Yes," she said, feeling flustered as she handed him the package.

Peter took it and unwrapped it. "My shoe!" he said in surprise.

"It is. I'm sorry. I took it. But I had a good reason," Alyssa said. She knew she likely wasn't making much sense, so she took a deep breath. "I needed it, to measure something."

"To measure? You had to measure something with my shoe?"

"That's right. You see, when I had tea with Laura and Maggie, Laura's table was wobbling."

"And you thought my shoe would fix it?" Peter sounded confused.

"No, no, I needed the shoe to...well, I know. I'm not making sense. Look at the bottom of the shoe," Alyssa asked.

He did. "There's an extra piece tacked on," he said.

"Right. So, the table was wobbling. And it reminded me of limping," Alyssa said, speaking quickly. She always did when she was nervous. "And Laura fixed it. With something at the bottom. So I thought..." she stopped. "Please don't be upset at me," she whispered. "I just want to help you. To stop your pain."

He gave her a puzzled look. "I am sorry. I just don't understand."

Alyssa's cheeks turned pink. Of course he didn't. She was jabbering away like a fool. "Put it on," she said. "And walk."

Peter removed the shoe he was wearing, and put on the other. They were similar enough it wasn't noticeable they were too different. He started to walk, then stopped.

"Keep going," Alyssa whispered. "Please."

He did. He walked, and then his face changed. It lit up. He looked down at his feet and laughed. "It works! This works! My leg doesn't hurt. I'm not limping."

Alyssa couldn't stop the smile that formed. Peter walked to her and pulled her into his arms. She was startled, but quickly relaxed into his too-short embrace. As he pulled back, she could have sworn there were tears in his eyes.

"Thank you," Peter said. "This is amazing. Incredible."

"The shoemaker said he can fix all of them, and can do that from here on," Alyssa said. "You just have to visit him."

"I will," Peter said, wonder in his voice. "To think...all these years, this could have been fixed with a simple bit of height added."

"Have you always struggled?" Alyssa asked, spreading out the blanket she'd brought to sit on.

"I was perhaps ten," Peter said, as he sat next to her. "I fell from a tree. When I broke my leg, it wasn't set right. As simple as that. And, so it appears, the fix is as well."

Her heart filled with pleasure. It felt good to have helped him. "You've done so much to help me," Alyssa said. "I just wanted to do something for you. I am so glad it was successful."

"More than successful," Peter said. He took her hands in his. "This is life changing."

Alyssa smiled at him. "I'm so glad."

A strange look came over Peter's face, and he stammered out something she didn't understand, as he pulled his hands back and reached into his pocket. He held out a piece of folded paper, and she noticed his hands were shaking.

"What's this?" Alyssa asked, as he offered it to her.

"I wrote this," Peter said. His voice was strange. Tight. Nervous. Beads of sweat formed on his temples. "Will you try to read it?"

Alyssa nodded. "I will." She unfolded the paper. After her lessons with Peter, she'd gotten much better. There were now several dozen words she knew, easily. What had he written her?

To her surprise, there wasn't much written on the paper. Just four words, carefully, neatly written.

She stilled. This couldn't be. Was she reading this correctly? Alyssa looked up at him. He looked terrified. The sight made her smile for some reason. "I am not sure if I am reading this correctly," she said softly, hoping he could hear her over the loud thumping of her heart. "Can I read it to you?"

He nodded. "Yes, of course."

Alyssa bit her lip and knew what she was about to read aloud would change everything. Forever.

Chapter 20

Peter's head was light. His stomach felt sick. He longed to reach into the cool stream and take a handful of the water to ease his discomfort, but he couldn't. Instead, his body was frozen. He was rooted to the spot and unable to move, just like the tall oak in town that they'd had to build the road around, because they couldn't remove it.

Alyssa's eyes were on the letter he'd written last night and carried around ever since. He almost hadn't given it to her, but he decided to act before thinking. And now, he hoped it was the right decision.

One way or another, everything was going to change.

"I..."

His eyes snapped to her face as she slowly read.

"Luh. Llluh. Lovvvuuh. Love."

Alyssa looked at him and he nodded, his mouth too dry to answer.

"I love you, Alyssa." She finished the words and looked at him.

"Yes," Peter said, and took her hands again. "I love you. I know you might not want a man like me—"

"A man like you?" she interrupted him. "One who is brave and patient, loving and kind? Who puts himself between me and danger? Of course, I do. I decided that I wasn't going to accept that other offer of marriage. It's you that I want. I just wasn't sure if you would want me in return. Now that I know, there's nothing I want more than to be here in Deepwater with you."

"Do you mean it?" Peter asked.

"Yes. I want to be with you forever, Peter. I want to read all of the books that you love and talk about them with you. I want to walk around town and visit this part of the stream with you, and always, always, have you because there is no one else that I want."

"That's just how I feel," Peter said. He looked deeply into her eyes. "I've never loved anyone before. You are my first, and my last, and my only, Alyssa Moore."

She smiled and moved closer. "West," she whispered.

"What's that?" Peter asked, confused.

"Soon I'll be Alyssa West. I think I'll like that name very much," she said with a smile.

"So will I," Peter agreed. Then he gently kissed her. As they separated, Alyssa's smile filled him with a joy he didn't think was possible.

"Maggie was right," Alyssa said suddenly.

"How so?" he answered.

"Deepwater. It has a way of pulling you in, and not letting you leave."

Peter pulled her back into his arms. "So do I."

As her laughter filled his ears and his heart, Peter knew there was nothing more that he wanted than for this moment to be forever.

Epilogue

Alyssa glanced at Peter. He had drifted off to sleep while she sketched the large tree surrounded by flowers in the garden the women of the town had recently created. Several men had built benches, and she found it was a place she enjoyed going to frequently. It was close to the stream, so there was so much beauty, it would be impossible not to enjoy the setting.

Smiling at her husband of only a few weeks, Alyssa leaned over and dropped a soft kiss on to his cheek. Peter's eyes fluttered open.

"Forgive me," he said, picking up the book he'd been holding. "I must have dozed off. It wasn't the company, I assure you."

She laughed. "I should think not," she answered, then looked critically at her sketch. "I'm nearly finished, then I'll head home to get dinner started."

"One more chapter then," Peter said and started to read. He'd only gotten a few sentences in when he stopped.

"What's wrong?" Alyssa asked.

"This is all so familiar," Peter said. "It's as though I dreamed it." Then he stilled. "I did dream this. This moment. By the stream, reading to you, and us happy. You," he reached over and took her hand. "You wearing a wedding ring."

"Is that so?" Alyssa asked. "What else did you dream?"

"I don't need to dream anything else ever again," Peter told her. "You are my dream, and have come true."

Alyssa smiled. He always said the sweetest kinds of things that made her heart glow. She picked up the book and slowly started to read it to the both of them. Her words were slow, but she was doing it. She had never felt more proud or happy than she did now.

During the mornings, she helped Maggie at the café. In the afternoons, she helped Peter at the post office, then they went home together. Her reading lessons continued, and the town had more than welcomed her into their embrace, as though she'd always been part of Deepwater.

Peter had taken all of his shoes to the shoemaker, and now walked painlessly, and more confidently. She reflected on how they'd each been just what the other needed.

She owed it, in part, to being rejected. That single act had forged a determination and confidence in her to take control of her own destiny.

As they walked home to their small house, Alyssa cast a glance at the stream. Peter noticed.

"What are you thinking about?" he asked her.

"I was thinking about Ophelia and Hamlet. How rejection is sometimes an opportunity. A chance for something better."

"It is," Peter agreed, finding her hand and squeezing it gently.

There was no need to say anything more. They walked in silence to their home, a place filled with warmth, and love, and good stories. Ones all of their choosing.

She hadn't enjoyed being rejected, but Alyssa couldn't deny that it had been the best thing ever to happen to her.

Return to Deepwater

Would you like to read about Laura and Gabriel (and the day they saved the town?) If you enjoyed this story, you might also like:

Trapped in Deepwater

Together, they are going to have to save themselves...and the town.

Laura Ashborne is convinced she's a walking bad luck charm. Trying to make a fresh start, she sets out on a stagecoach to become a schoolteacher. However, the coach she's on breaks down in the middle of nowhere a few days before Christmas, and she's forced to spend an entire week in the tiny town of Deepwater.

Reverend Gabriel Sullivan wants to help the beautiful stranded traveler, and he'd determined to show her she's not bad luck. But when his dark past catches up to him, he's put into a dangerous situation, and Laura right along with him.

Can her desperate plan help him? Or will they let their past ruin the future they'd like to have together?

Find it on Amazon:

https://www.amazon.com/Trapped-Deepwater-Christmas-Bride-Dilemma-ebook/dp/B0C74R6NW6

Curious about the tailor who needs a wife? His story will appear in 2025, in Mail-Order Tailor when he makes his way to Deepwater.

Note from Author

Thank you for taking the time to read Alyssa's Desperate Plan!

Could I ask for one small favor? Reviews like yours on Amazon mean so much to me and help others to find my books! Even just a single line means a lot!

Also...

Want a FREE book?

Stop by my website to get your no strings attached **FREE book**. It's my gift to you, as a thank you for reading this one.

www.sarahlambbooks.com

Note from Author

Thank you for reading *Alyssa's Desperate Plan.*

Could I ask for one small favor? Reviews like yours on Amazon mean so much to me and help others to find my books! Even just a single line means a lot!

About the Author

Sarah is wife to an amazing teacher and mom to two boys who are growing up just a little too fast. She spends her days working and writing in the Blue Ridge Mountains and planning her next trip to Disney World.

Get Your Free Book

Want a FREE book?

Stop by my website to get your no strings attached **FREE book**. It's my gift to you, as a thank you for reading this one.

www.sarahlambbooks.com

There are other great books in this series as well!

Find all the Rejected Mail-Order Bride books on Amazon!

https://www.amazon.com/dp/B0CN8C625X

Want more of Sarah's books? She writes for children and adults! Find them all on Amazon!

https://www.amazon.com/stores/Sarah-Lamb/author/B098H3SGLK

www.ingramcontent.com/pod-product-compliance
Lightning Source LLC
Chambersburg PA
CBHW022129170626
46808CB00002B/912